julie and romeo

julie

and

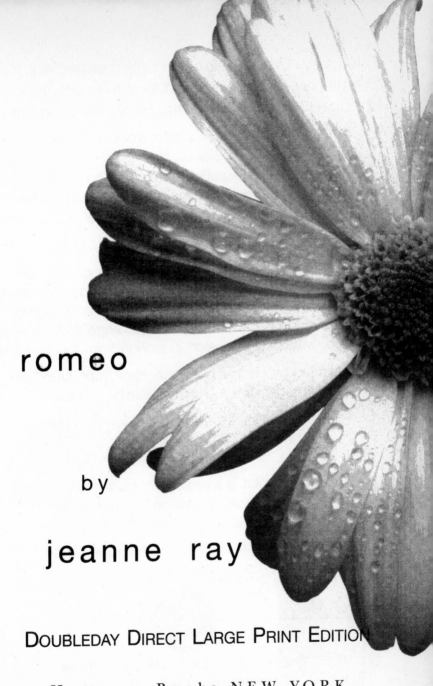

romeo

by

jeanne ray

DOUBLEDAY DIRECT LARGE PRINT EDITION

Harmony Books NEW YORK

This Large Print Edition, prepared especially for Doubleday Direct, Inc., contains the complete, un-abridged text of the original Publisher's Edition.

PUBLISHER'S NOTE: This is a work of fiction. The names, characters, places, and incidents either are the product of the author's imagination or are used fictitiously, and any resemblance to actual persons, living or dead, events, or locales is entirely coincidental.

Published by Harmony Books, New York, New York. Member of the Crown Publishing Group.

Random House, Inc. New York, Toronto, London, Sydney, Auckland
www.randomhouse.com

Harmony Books is a registered trademark and the Harmony Books colophon is a trademark of Random House, Inc.

Printed in the United States of America

ISBN 0-7394-1079-2

**This Large Print Book carries the
Seal of Approval of N.A.V.H.**

For Darrell
I love you all

"What's in a name?
That which we call a rose
By any other word
would smell as sweet."
—WILLIAM SHAKESPEARE,
Romeo and Juliet

julie and romeo

chapter one

The first time I heard the name Cacciamani I was five years old. My father said it, and then he spit. The spitting I had seen before. I watched my father spit out his toothpaste into the sink. I had seen him spit once while mowing the lawn when he claimed to have taken in a mouthful of gnats. But this particular spitting, the spitting done in association with the word *Cacciamani,* was done directly onto the cement floor of the back room of Roseman's, our family's florist shop. That floor, like everything else in my father's world, was kept meticulously clean, nary a leaf hit that floor, and so even as a child I recognized the utter seriousness of his gesture.

"Pigs," my father said, referring not to himself for what he had done to his floor but to the name that had led him to do it.

I wish I could remember the rest of this story, how the Cacciamanis had come up in the first place, but I was five. Fifty-five years later, only the highlights of such childhood memories remain.

Commentators, the people reading their opinions on the news, the people on the op-ed page of the *Globe*, love to say that hate is a learned thing. Children mimic the appalling racial slurs of their appalling parents, every bitter, contemptible piece of narrow-mindedness is handed down from generation to generation like so much fine family silver. I doubt it is as easy as this, as I know my own two daughters have picked up a few things in this world I will not take responsibility for, but then I think of my father and the small, shimmery pool of his spit on the floor. I hated Cacciamani with all the passionate single-mindedness of a child without even knowing what or who it was. I decided it was a fish. My father, who loved just about everything, was not a fan of fish, and so I assumed the conversation must have gone something like this:

MY MOTHER: Howard, I got some
   nice fresh Cacciamani for dinner
   tonight.
MY FATHER: Cacciamani! [Spit] Pigs!

For the next several years I imagined pale-fleshed, rubbery bottom feeders, the dreaded Cacciamani, snuffling around blindly at the bottom of Boston Harbor. No doubt my mother intended to fry them and serve them up in a buttery lemon sauce.

When exactly I made the transition from fish to family, from family to rival florists, I don't know (again, remember, this was the distant past). It hardly ruled my life. My path did not cross with the Cacciamanis', and when it did, they had to be pointed out to me like a patch of poison ivy I could have walked right into. We did not go to the same school. Their son went to the idol-worshiping, uniform-wearing Catholic school, while my brother and I attended perfectly normal public school. Their name was rarely spoken and when it was there was a great fanfare of unexplained wrath that I gladly participated in. We were a liberal family, aware of the recent persecution of our people and therefore unlikely to persecute others. As far as I knew, the only prejudice we had was against the Cacciamanis. It didn't extend to other Catholics or all Italians, just those people, those wretched, worthless fish. A prejudice can be a lovely thing to have, which is exactly why so many people have them in the first place. A prejudice is a simplification: Every member of this group is exactly the same and therefore I never have to think about any of them. What a time-saver! Of course, it didn't save me much time because back then there were only three Cacciamanis for me to hate, a father, a mother, and the son. I remember seeing the mother at Haymarket several times on Saturdays. She was beautiful, tall and thin, with black hair and red lips. Still, I thought it was an evil sort of beauty. Then their son grew up, married, and had six children, many of whom married and had children of their own. The Cacciamani clan grew by leaps and bounds and as far as I was concerned the whole lot of them were worthless, a fact that was reinforced when Tony Cacciamani tried to marry my daughter Sandy when they were in high school.

So that was how I came to hate Cacciamanis. Now let me tell you how I stopped. It was five years ago when I came to hate my husband, Mort. Mort ran off with Lila, the thirty-eight-year-old bouquet-grasping bridesmaid he met at a wedding while delivering flowers. Apparently he met her at several weddings. She was practically a professional bridesmaid, many friends, few dates. There went Mort and Lila. After that I knew what it was to really hate someone on your own terms, for your own reasons, which is much more poignant than hating on someone else's behalf. I didn't know I had ceased to carry an axe for the Cacciamanis. There was no conscious moment: I hate Mort and so expunge the record of the Cacciamanis. I simply hadn't thought of them for years. And then one day, while attending a seminar at the downtown Boston Sheraton called "Making Your Small Business Thrive," I practically walked into a man with the name tag ROMEO CACCIAMANI. I probably would have recognized his face, but I saw the name first. I steeled myself for the great wave of fury that was surely coming. I planted my feet and took a breath, but nothing, not even a twinge. What came instead was this thought: Poor

Romeo Cacciamani; his shop must be going bust, too, if he's at this thing.

He tilted his head a little and squinted at me. I think Romeo Cacciamani needed glasses. "Julie Roseman," he said, reading my tag.

And there he was, a nice-looking Italian guy sitting right at sixty. He was wearing pressed khaki pants and a white polo shirt with a sprig of chest hair flourishing at the throat. No gold chains. I was so surprised by my utter lack of hostility that I wanted to laugh. I wanted to shake his hand, and I would have except I had a Styrofoam cup of hot coffee in one hand and several folders of tax spreadsheets and workmen's comp advice in the other. "Romeo Cacciamani," I said with wonder.

"It was something else, wasn't it? Roth?"

I nodded. "Roth," I said. "And Roth no more."

He raised his eyebrows in a not-unfriendly way, as if he should be shocked and wasn't. Something occurred to me then: Did Cacciamanis still hate the Rosemans? I knew that Mort and Romeo had gotten into it over the years, but now Mort was gone and my parents were dead and my younger brother, scarcely a Roseman at all, was making twig furniture in Montana. That left me and my daughters, Sandy and Nora. "Are your parents . . ."

"My father's been gone"—he lifted his eyes to the acoustical ceiling of the conference hall as if the answer might have been contained there—"eleven years now? Ten? My mother lives with me. Almost ninety. When is the last time I saw you?"

No sooner had he said it than he remembered the answer to his own question. I could see the edges of his ears turn red. "Fifteen years," I said, and left it at that. That was the last time we had seen each other, but that was not the last time I had seen him. Over the years I had seen Romeo plenty, as we drove past each other in our cars, as I turned my grocery cart into his aisle at Demoula's and then caught the mistake in time and wheeled off in the other direction. You know what they say, "See you later"—"Not if I see you first." For all I knew, he had been studiously avoiding me as well. We both lived in Somerville, which is hardly a bustling metropolis but a big enough place to avoid someone for years. We owned the only two florist shops in town, so it stood to reason that if one of us was providing the flowers for a wedding or funeral, the other one wouldn't be there.

"How's Sandy?" he said.

"She's good," I said. He was a better person than I was. I wasn't going to be asking about his Tony.

"Things turned out for her okay?"

I shrugged. "You have kids. You know how it is. Her marriage didn't work out. She's back home with me now. Two children." I felt awkward. I wanted to say everything was fantastic for her, a lifetime of happiness and she never looked back for a second. I wanted to say it not for myself but for Sandy, who, in her weaker moments, still felt the loss of Tony Cacciamani.

He scratched the top of his head, where all of his hair appeared to be intact. "That was a sad thing," he said, as much to himself as to me. "A very sad thing. What my son was doing with a Roseman—"

"A Roth," I corrected. "Sandy was a Roth."

Romeo smiled. "You're all Rosemans as far as I'm concerned. And your husband was the biggest Roseman of them all."

So at least that answered that question.

We were not fighting our battle alone. "My husband only looked like a Roseman. In the end he proved to be otherwise."

"I'm sorry to hear that."

"I'm better off," I said, though my very presence at this seminar of hopelessness proved otherwise, at least on the business front. "He met somebody else." I don't know what possessed me to include this last bit of information, but once it was said, there was no taking it back.

Romeo nodded sadly. Maybe he thought he'd known what kind of guy Mort was all along, or maybe he felt sorry for me, but either way I knew it was time for our reunion to come to an end. "I need to get going," I said, struggling to get a look at my watch. "I want to get a seat for the advertising panel."

He let me go graciously, said something about it being nice to see me again. Had he always had such a nice face?

"Romeo?" I said. I don't think I had ever called him by his first name. It was always "Mr. Cacciamani" even though we were the same age. I had never wanted to appear familiar, and besides, I thought Romeo was a ridiculous name for an adult. He stopped and turned back to me. "I read in the paper about your wife. I was sorry about that." It was so long ago, three years, four? After Mort left, I know. I should have sent a card at least.

He nodded a little. "Thank you."

"I didn't know her. I mean, I think I only met her that one time, but I had a lot of respect for her. She seemed like a lovely woman."

"Camille was a lovely woman," he said sadly, and then he turned away.

After the panel moderator announced that it was essential for every small-business owner to set aside ten percent of his or her gross revenues for advertising, I stopped listening. A great idea, unless you plan to make payroll or have dinner every now and then. Instead my mind drifted back to something Romeo had said about Mort being the biggest Roseman of all. It hit the nail on the head, and I wondered how a Cacciamani could have so much insight into my life. The whole time I was growing up I worked in my parents' shop. Even as a little girl I was sitting in the back room filling up the stik-piks or wrapping florist tape around the bottom of corsages. When I got older, my father moved me out front to work the cash register, and when I was in college, I came in early to do the arrangements for the day. I loved the shop when I was young, the cool, dark world of the walk-in on a hot summer day, the bright yellow light of an African daisy in February. I loved the lush piles of discarded leaves in the trash cans and the constant, dizzying perfume of the gardenias. But then I met Mort and he started hanging around the store, so helpful, so polite. From our second date my mother was saying, When is he going to marry you? Like he'd been stringing me along for years and I was about to let my best chance get away. I was all of twenty-one, just minutes away from being yesterday's fresh pick. Six months later Mort asked my father if he could marry me, which might have been construed as charming and old-fashioned, but nobody asked me anything. Me they told. "Julie, Julie!" my mother said when I walked in the store, and my father's eyes were beaming from all the tears and Mort was just standing there, a grinning idiot, like I was going to be so proud of him. It was a good ten minutes before I could figure out what in the hell was going on. They'd sold me off, or at least that's what it felt like. My brother, Jake, had bailed out on the business and in Mort they had found a responsible son to assume the Roseman mantle. I was nothing but the conduit for the transaction. But this isn't the truth. This is my memory speaking. I am telling the beginning of the story when I am the one who knows the end. I'm sure I was happy at the time. I have a vague idea that I loved Mort then.

I made my own bouquet for the wedding. My parents did everything else, but the bouquet was mine—white tuberoses, white hydrangeas, white peonies, and a few orange blossoms for luck. It was the most beautiful work I'd ever done, good enough for Grace Kelly, and I wrapped a silky white ribbon around the stems. Then at the end of the reception I walked up a few stairs at the front of the banquet hall. The band was playing "Satin Doll" and everyone was yelling, "Throw it! Throw it!" All my single girlfriends were there: Gloria, my maid of honor, all the bridesmaids, such a pretty semicircle of well-wishers. I turned my back on them and with all my might I threw my beautiful bouquet up over my head. The flowers sailed right out of my hands. It was nearly thirty-five years before I got them back again.

Mort didn't want me in the shop. This was rule number one when we got back from our honeymoon. My parents agreed. They could only afford one employee, and since Mort would be taking over sooner or later what mattered was that he learn the business. I could use my college education working as a secretary for an insurance company with the understanding that I would quit work as soon as I got pregnant. Nobody was drugging me. Nobody put a gun to my head. That was just the way things went, and it didn't even seem strange to me then. Marriage, babies, long afternoons ironing shirts and watching daytime television—those were all the things I aspired to anyway. Mort became the Roseman and I became his wife. Who would have believed it was my name on the front of the store and not his? When people called the house and asked for Mr. Roseman, I just handed him the phone. It was a beautiful name, a florist's name, why shouldn't he want it?

My parents retired safe in the knowledge that Mort was there and they died before he got around to proving them wrong. For this

I am grateful. At least he didn't cause my parents any pain. To say they loved him like a son would be something of an under-statement and I think his departure would have been a greater blow to them than it was even to me. But for all their love and unquestioning trust, they did one very strange thing: They left me the shop. Me. Just me, everything in my name. Mort cursed and raged for weeks. "What a slap!" he said. "A betrayal!" I didn't understand what he was talking about. It wasn't like they left it to my brother, who got the savings and the assets from the sale of their house.

"It's ours," I said. "My name, your name, what difference does it make?"

Mort said it made a difference, a big dif-ference, and soon he was after me to sign over the title. While I've done a lot of dumb things in my life, I am pleased to report that this wasn't one of them. He groused. I stalled. He left. It turns out Lila had her eye on my parents' shop. Mort and Lila's Flow-ers. The very thought of it makes me weak.

A lot can change in thirty-five years. While I was driving car pools and taking Nora and Sandy to tap and ballet classes, the world of flowers was moving forward. I volunteered

at adult literacy centers, worked on my overhead serve, and perfected the art of stuffing
fresh herbs beneath the skin of a chicken,
but I didn't learn one thing about the business. Sure, I went into the shop from time
to time. I dropped things off or picked things
up. I helped myself to a bunch of roses if we
were having a dinner party. But I was surprised one day when I noticed that the cash
register was a computer and no one had told
me about it. Shipping, billing, trucking,
taxes—the depth of my ignorance was bot-
tomless. I had never noticed that we now
sold fancy ribbon and vases. There was even
a wire rack of greeting cards beside the door.
Mort didn't leave a manual when he and Lila
packed off for Seattle. Nor did he leave
much money. He just left.

What a beautiful story this would be if the
wronged wife pulled it out of the fire and took
the business straight to the *Fortune 500*. I
believed that I would be doing the arrangements for the Ritz-Carlton lobby in no time.
It didn't work out that way. I stayed in bed
for a while and when I got up I found a lot
of rotted flowers and unpaid bills. I couldn't
sell the store. It had been my parents' entire
life, and as little as I knew about flowers, I

knew less about just about everything else. I went to work.

Five years later I was spending money I didn't have on a seminar that was telling me to put ten percent into advertising. I still thought there was some piece of information out there that would make all the difference. If only I knew what I should be doing, it would all turn out okay. My hips were getting stiff in the folding chair and my coffee was cold. All around me desperate losers like myself were taking frantic notes. Fortunately I had taken a spot at the back of the auditorium and so I could creep out without too much embarrassment. I pushed open the heavy metal fire door and slipped into the hallway. It was empty except for an orange bench on which sat one Romeo Cacciamani.

The first time I saw Romeo in the Sheraton, I was amazed to find I no longer hated him. The second time I saw him, I was considerably more amazed to find my heart jumped up as if there had been a tiny trampoline installed in my chest. Was he waiting for me?

He glanced up at me and then looked down at his hands. "Oh," he said, his voice

disappointed. "You've got coffee. I was going to ask you if you wanted a cup of coffee."

I looked at him and then at the white cup
in my hand. There wasn't a trash can, so I
dug it into the sand of a very clean ashtray.
"I'd like a cup of coffee," I said.

chapter two

Romeo Cacciamani held open the door of the downtown Boston Sheraton for me and I stepped outside into a beautiful late spring day. There were a million things that should have been going through my head: Why has he asked me for coffee? Does he want to talk about what happened with the kids? Does he want to talk about business? Is he going to tell me he hates me in the fine tradition of his family? But in truth the only thing I was thinking was, Wouldn't Mort just die? Please, God, let Mort be in Boston for the weekend. Let him be in a coffee shop across the street watching me smile and shake my hair out in the sunlight while Romeo Cacciamani looks on attentively. Let Mort see everything and think that we are wildly in love and that I am planning on signing over every last petal I have to this man. Nothing would kill Mort faster.

"Starbucks okay?" Romeo said, looking down the street.

I told him that was fine.

We found a table among the full-time students and unemployed writers who believed that coffee shops were libraries. Romeo paid for my light grande latte decaf and got himself a cup of black coffee. I found myself wishing I had asked for black coffee, too.

"Two bucks for a cup of coffee," he said, sinking into his chair. "Why didn't I think of that one? I've got plenty of coffee."

"Beanie Babies," I said. "I should have come up with those."

"We sell them at the store," he said. "I hate them. People call all day long, 'Do you have Spots? Do you have Gobbler?' We had to put in an extra line so the flower calls can come through."

Not only had I not thought of making Beanie Babies in time, I hadn't even thought of selling them. "So business must be good."

He glanced down at our mutual stack of

small-business folders. "You know how it is."

The thought seemed to depress us both and for a while we just sipped our coffee in silence.

"I've thought over the years maybe I should write to you," Romeo said. "It's the kind of thing you think about, but then, who does it? And then I saw you today and I thought—"

But he stopped, not saying what he thought, and after a while I was too curious to wait politely. "What would you write to me about?"

"Oh, all of this." He gestured an open hand at the table, and for a minute I thought he'd wanted to write to me about coffee. "The family stuff, the thing between our families." He stopped and shook his head. "Sandy. I wanted to write to you about Sandy. Or maybe I should have written to Sandy. I look back on all that and I think I just didn't . . . I didn't handle that whole thing so well. All the yelling and Camille crying, all the back and forth. I still think they were too young to get married, even though Camille and I weren't too much older than they were when we did it. It may have been okay to bust up the wedding, but I don't think we should have busted *them* up. That was about us, not about them."

It was a terrible night, freezing cold and pouring down rain. Tony Cacciamani had actually brought a ladder to our house like Sandy was some sort of hostage. She was going to climb down the ladder and they were going to get married, but the ladder fell and there was Sandy, hanging off the sill of her second-story bedroom window, screaming. We had said it was all a Cacciamani plot, that Tony was really trying to kill Sandy.

"That was a long time ago," I said. And it was, but it made me sad to even think about it.

He nodded. "A long time. I have one daughter. I don't know if you know that. Plummy. She's the last one. She's at Boston College now. Such a smart kid, Jesus, I wonder where she came from. She's not like anybody else in the family. But when all that happened with Sandy and Tony, my Plummy was just a little girl, barely even walking around. I didn't know anything about girls then."

I was remembering Sandy, sixteen years old, up on her bed crying and crying and Tony Cacciamani calling the house all the time and Mort hanging up on him. Mort told Sandy he had never called her. Then we sent her off on a foreign-exchange program to Sweden and she got such a terrible case of mono that the host family sent her back to us two months later. I never thought about it anymore. It was a dark chapter in my parenting history. "I understand," I said. "We don't have to talk about this." Anyone who knows me knows that "We don't have to talk about this" is a very simplistic code for "Stop talking about this." Romeo did not know the code.

"What I mean to say is that now Plummy is a young lady, grown-up, very pretty like her mother."

I nodded, though in my memory Camille was not so pretty.

"I think I have a better understanding now of how it must have looked from your side. If Plummy were to tell me she was getting married to anybody, much less a Roseman . . . Well, it's just more complicated when you have daughters." He leaned in toward me, almost whispering to keep the writers from listening in. "When you have boys you think that all the world's problems come from girls. You start thinking bad things about all the girls. Then you have a girl, and man, you start to take another look at all the boys out there. The world starts looking like a dangerous place."

That made me laugh. I tried to snap myself out of the past. "Kids are going to make mistakes," I said. "Big mistakes. All we can do is teach them what's best and then stand by to bail them out."

"Well, that's what you did. You protected your daughter. That's what I would have said in that letter I didn't write to you."

"We didn't do such a great job ourselves, you know. We weren't exactly models of civility. Mort said some awful things about Tony, about you. God, I remember the screaming that went on then." I tried to remember what I thought about Romeo Cacciamani all those years ago when he and his wife sat on our couch. Was he nice? Was he bright? Did I think he was a good-looking guy? I wasn't sure. Was it possible that he had simply become such a good-looking guy in the last fifteen years?

"He hated us. That was for sure. Mort

Roseman's daughter sneaking off with a Cacciamani." He shook his head. "That's powerful stuff."

"Roth," I reminded him. "Mort Roth."

Romeo shrugged.

"I hated you, too," I said, and then was, for the second time since we had met, horrified by my own sudden inclination toward candidness.

But as far as Romeo was concerned I hadn't confessed anything more serious than a dislike for decaf. "Cacciamanis and Rosemans," he said. "Very bad blood."

I saw this as my opportunity to get the answer to a question that had been bothering me for years, one that I could never ask my father or mother or husband because it was surely too obvious and I was too stupid. "Why do we hate each other?"

"I'm not sure, to tell you the truth." Romeo took a long drink of his coffee, not seeming to mind that it was still steaming hot. "After Tony and Sandy got together, I could say it was because of what happened to them, but certainly I hated all of you a long time before that. My parents hated your parents. Whew!" He shook his head. "Now that was hate. My mother crept into your parents' yard one night and poured salt on the roots of all your mother's roses."

"She killed the roses? Are you kidding me? My mother always said it was some kind of Cacciamani curse." They had simply withered up, every last one of them, and after that she couldn't make a single thing grow there. Finally my father bought some flagstones and just covered up the dirt.

"It was Cacciamani table salt. Maybe the same thing. One time, I must have been in about the eighth grade, and I had gone to a birthday party and you were there. I didn't talk to you or anything, I knew better than that, but at dinner that night I told my father that I thought you were sort of cute and he dragged me to the bathroom by my collar and washed my mouth out with soap. Ever had your mouth washed out with soap?"

I shook my head.

"It's disgusting. Truly."

I tried to assume the least coquettish tone possible. I tried to make my voice sound like Dan Rather's. "So you thought I was cute?" I had some attributes left, but it had been a long time since anyone had used the word *cute* in conjunction with my name.

"I was at that age. I was trying to hack my father off, even though I didn't know it would hack him off that much." He took another sip of coffee and looked out the window. "But yeah, I thought you were cute then. Actually, I think you're cute now."

Let me establish something here: Things had not been so hot between me and Mort in the years before he left. We had been in a long decline. Since Mort, nothing. I was not proud of this. It was not the way I would have wished for things to happen, but that's the way it was, and I had no idea what to do about it. I had no time to do anything about it, not between working around the clock and taking care of the house and helping Sandy out with her kids. I would need so many seminars on dating that I would never have known where to begin. And yes, there were times that people flirted with me, a man coming in to buy flowers for his wife, the lonely trucker who brings me my flowers. I wouldn't have done it and they probably didn't mean it, anyway. But a real compliment, a genuinely kind word from a seemingly nice man, well, that hadn't happened for a very long time. It was like a faint song. Something sweet and far away.

"I don't remember you at a party," I said. "I wish I did."

He waved his hand. "I was a very cool kid." He smiled. His teeth lapped over one another a little bit, but they were nice teeth. "I came and stood around the edges for a minute, then I left. That was my style."

As much as I wanted to see where this might go, I couldn't get my mind off the salt. "So why did your mother kill our roses?"

"That part I could not tell you. I always thought you knew. The way they said the word *Roseman* around our house, you would have thought there had been a whole bunch of murder and extortion somewhere along the line."

"I don't think my parents killed any Cacciamanis."

"What about your grandparents?"

"Jews in Lithuania. They didn't get to Italy much. I hear the train service was very bad. But your mother is still alive, can't you ask her?"

"Salting the roses is what I *know* she did; the things I don't know, I wouldn't want to know. My mother is a tough lady. She would be capable of some pretty serious stuff. If she hasn't told me by now why she hated the Rosemans, she's never going to tell me."

"What about your kids?"

Romeo drummed his fingers on the top of the table. He had nice hands, thin and strong like maybe he played the piano. He still wore his wedding ring. "I'm afraid that one is my fault."

"Ah, don't worry about it. Mort and I didn't exactly talk you up to our girls over dinner."

"They hate us?"

Nora hated. Nora with her Lexus and her cell phone, her tax attorney husband and blisteringly hot real-estate career, Nora hated the Cacciamanis with a passion that would rival anyone in the family. She was a daddy's girl. She would walk out of her best friend's wedding if the Cacciamanis had done the flowers. Sandy hated them, too, but for her own reasons. Sandy hated them because she really did love Tony. She named her little boy Tony, which I thought was a very questionable move, but I never said a word about it. "They hate you."

"My boys, they act like boys. They get a grudge and that's it, real Cacciamanis all of them. Plummy I'm not so sure about. She does her studies, she dances, she works in the shop. I don't think she's got time to hate anybody."

You hear people talk about someone lighting up. I've always thought it was a silly turn of phrase, as if we all came with concealed electrical cords, but when Romeo spoke of his daughter he actually seemed to throw off light.

"So you don't seem to hate me and I don't seem to hate you," he said. "What do you think happened to us?"

I explained what had happened, at least to me. How I hated along the family lines but then things changed for me. I told him about Mort. I told him that if someone had asked me how I felt about the Cacciamanis while I was eating my shredded wheat this morning, I would have said something awful out of the sheer reflexive habit of it all, but that when I saw him, just another failing small-business owner like myself, it all seemed to be gone.

He was a good listener. He held very still when I talked and looked right at me. "I understand," he said. "When Camille died—" He stopped for a minute, tapped his cup against the table a few times as if hoping to say it in code. "Well, I changed my mind about a lot of things. I would have been happy to have her forever, to go on hating the Rosemans like always, but it didn't work out that way. I lost Camille and I lost all my energy for trivial things. I inherited her good sense when she died. She willed it to me."

"That's quite a gift."

"Quite a gift," Romeo repeated slowly. "So really, it's not so different. We both lost the person we loved and the hate just went with it."

"It's not the same. I didn't love Mort. Not like you loved Camille."

"Nobody loves the same way, but you loved Mort. You must have. Otherwise you wouldn't have stayed with the idiot for so many years."

I laughed and Romeo laughed and then he put his fine slender hand over my wrist and patted it. It was not a sexual sort of thing—I certainly recognized it as a friendly gesture—but it was nice, a little touch.

He picked up our cups and my crumpled-up napkins and put them all in the trash. When we stepped outside the sun was still bright and the air was crisp and as sweet as hyacinth. Romeo Cacciamani raised up on his toes a couple of times and bounced a little. "The lecture on self-employed retirement accounts starts at three," he said.

"So what, I could contribute for another five years. What good is that going to do me? I don't have any money for a self-employed retirement account. Besides, I'm never going to be able to retire."

"Me neither," he said. "Too many kids."

"How many kids?"

"Six. The five boys and Plummy."

I whistled.

"So, no more lectures. I guess it's back

to Somerville." He looked down the street as if he were expecting a car to pull up and take him home. "You drive?"

"Are you crazy? Parking was a fortune. I took the bus."

He nodded and again he scanned the street for his ride, looking as far away from me as possible. "Ever walk to Somerville?"

"From downtown?"

He nodded. "I noticed your shoes. You wear sensible shoes. You could walk in those."

I had given up on sexy shoes back when the girls were born. I was extremely, irrationally flattered to think that he had looked at my feet. "I'm a florist," I said. "I stand up all day."

"But you told your family you were going to be at the seminar till at least five, right? You have plenty of time still."

"I don't think I've ever walked that far in my life."

"It isn't that bad. You walk that far every day just around the store. I do. Let's say we give it a try and if it doesn't work we split the cab back."

There was no sign of rain and I had had the good sense to leave my folders on the table in Starbucks. There had been a freak snowstorm in April, but every last bit of slush and gray ice had melted away. The sidewalks looked clear and dry, appropriate for travel. I nodded. Where had I come to in my life that walking from Boston to Somerville could seem like an act of wanton recklessness? "Sure," I said. "Hell, yes."

And so we started back, out of the shadow of the Prudential Center and off toward Mass. Ave. We made the very, very long trip over the Mass. Ave. bridge, where the sky reflected pink light into the Charles River and off to the right the last of the day's sailboats skated across the water. Who knew that walking to Somerville could be such a beautiful thing to do? I have not been to Paris, but I can't imagine it's a whole lot better than this. It was a longer trip than we expected, and when we started to get tired, Romeo suggested we stop in La Groceria and have a plate of spaghetti for dinner. They had a very nice bottle of not so expensive Chianti. What was funny was we didn't much talk about our families. We talked about movies and a hospital show on television that we both liked. We talked about growing up in Boston and the trips we had taken and the trips we had always meant to take. After dinner we walked for a long time without saying anything at all. It was pretty, looking at the houses at dusk, all the warm orange light coming from the front windows. I liked to imagine the people inside, to wonder about how their lives had turned out and whether they were happy or disappointed. It didn't bother me, not talking to Romeo. I never felt that we were two people who had run out of things to say, but that we were two people who knew each other well. Two people who had nothing but time.

chapter three

As soon as I saw the silvery Lexus parked in the driveway, I knew I was in serious trouble. I was late. I had forgotten that it was Sandy's night for school and I was supposed to be watching the kids. She must have waited and waited and finally called her sister as a last possible resort for child care. I sat down on the low brick wall around my little front yard and took a breath, wanting to put off for a moment what I knew was coming. I loved Nora, but she was a force to be reckoned with. She did not tolerate forgetfulness nor suffer inconvenience gladly. I wanted just a minute to think about my happy evening, the good food, the long walk home. Romeo, thankfully, had veered off toward his own home and live-in relatives five blocks ago, trusting that I was enough of an adult to find my way back in safety. I would not have wanted him to see me like this, hiding from my daughter in my yard. Who could have thought a person could walk all the way from downtown Boston? I had lived here my whole life and the thought had never even crossed my mind.

I fished out my keys from the bottom of my purse, touched my fingers to my lips to make sure I wasn't wearing any bread crumbs, and then I went inside. Nora had every light in the house blazing. My grand-children Tony and Sarah, eight and four re-spectively, were both up. They were both crying.

"My God!" Nora said, coming toward me like a train. "I was just telling the children I was going to have to call the police. Mother, where have you been? I was absolutely sure you were d-e-a-d."

"You were dead!" Sarah wailed, and shim-mied up into my arms. My back is not the back it once was. Tony banded himself around my waist and began to squeeze.

I tried to steady myself beneath the weight. "I'm not dead. Shush, stop crying. Look at me." I pulled her chin back. Such a wealth of tears! "Look at me. See, do I look dead to you?"

She thought for a second and then shook her head, but the crying had taken on a life of its own and could not be stopped. She was making a gasping, choking sob that sounded something like *naagha, naagha.* I rubbed small circles on her back. "Tony," I said, looking down on the crown of his head. "Are you all right?"

Tony, never much of a talker, nodded into my waist, moving around an extra ten pounds I should lose. The whole thing broke my heart. Really, these kids killed me. There was so much passion in their fear. I looked at Nora, who spread her hands open as if to say, Look at all the suffering you've caused.

"I just forgot," I said. "I forgot it was Sandy's school night or I would have come straight home."

"So where were you?" Nora said.

I felt very bad, yes, very guilty. I was quite literally stained with the tears of these children, but I was not too crazed with the whole thing that I could not see the irony of my situation. As far as I know, Sandy tried to get married once in high school, and other than that she was up in her room watching television. Nora, on the other hand, put us through hell, staying out until four in the morning, saying she was running down the street for a Coke and coming back six hours later on the back of some boy's motorcycle. I found her film canister of pot in her sock drawer and her diaphragm case taped to the bottom of the clothes hamper. This well-dressed real-estate broker with the lizard shoes and the diamond stud earrings who folded her arms across her chest had been grounded more times than I could count. Grounded by me, her mother. "I went to the seminar. I ran into a friend. We had dinner and walked home."

"Walked home! From the Sheraton! I'm sitting here with these children thinking you're dead—"

At the word *dead,* Sarah began to wail again.

"—and you're walking to Somerville!"

"If I had *remembered,* I wouldn't have walked home." Enough was enough. I put Sarah down and peeled Tony off of me. They tottered toward the sofa, drunk with their grief. "Nora, I'm sorry you had to come over here and I thank you for your help with the children." I tried to put the mother-note of authority back into my voice, not that it had ever meant a thing to her, anyway.

Then Nora's husband, Alex, appeared in the front hall holding a sandwich in a paper towel. I appreciated his impulse toward neatness. "Hey, hey," he said, "look what the cat dragged in." Either he did not believe I was dead or he didn't care.

"I forgot, Alex. I'm sorry."

"She *walked* home from the *Sheraton,*" Nora said.

He nodded, gave me a thumbs-up, and went back toward the television. "They say it's even better for you than running if you go far enough."

"Why did you bring Alex?" I asked Nora. I was much more comfortable inconveniencing my daughter than I was her husband, which probably represented some narrow, sexist impulse in my thinking.

"We were on our way out the door to dinner when Sandy called. She said you were only going to be a few minutes late. She didn't tell me she hadn't even heard from you."

"I'm sorry."

"We had reservations at Biba."

I didn't know what that was, but I apologized again, hopefully for the last time.

Alex finished his sandwich and the children returned to their normal breathing patterns and fell into an exhausted stupor on the floor. Nora put on her coat, which was cut like a trench coat but was made from a pale yellow silk that looked simply lovely on her. I never could get over the way Nora had turned out, so successful, so striking, so, frankly, rich. In my wildest dreams I wouldn't have guessed it, not when she had been such an utter hellion. Never write off a kid who gives you bunches of trouble—I suppose that's the moral of the story. "You look so nice," I said.

"Well, we were going out." Nora shrugged and lifted her dark hair over the collar of her coat. Then she smiled at me, maybe to indicate that she was over it. "It's okay. I forget things, too."

Slightly patronizing but I'd take it.

"Who did you run into, anyway?"

I laughed at the thought of it, the whole happy absurdity. "You'd never guess. Never in a million years would you believe who I had dinner with."

Nora returned my happy look, picking up her purse. It was a little game. "Who?"

"Romeo Cacciamani. Can you believe that?"

I should have thought this over and lied. Just because I had run into the enemy of all Rosemans and found nothing in my heart but peace did not mean that such peace would be shared by all members of my tribe.

Nora dropped her purse. Maybe she was being overly dramatic or maybe she was freeing up her hands to strangle me. "You *what?* You did *what?*"

Tony and Sarah, even in their diminished states, heard the shift in tone and raised their sleepy heads up from the carpet. Alex came over with a look of real alarm on his face.

"What?" he said, and the word was mimicked by the children.

"Nora," I said quietly. "Go home. We can talk about this some other time."

"Tell me!" Nora said. Nora actually roared. She was capable of that.

I kept my voice very soft, but there was no undoing this. "I ran into Romeo Cacciamani at the conference. We got to talking, we had dinner."

"Cacciamani? You ate dinner with a Cacciamani?"

It was amazing. She sounded exactly like her grandfather when she said the word. I half expected her to spit.

I was trying to think what I would have said if Nora had run into a Cacciamani and not me. Would I still be willing to raise the torch in anger? "I asked myself, What was this huge feud all about, anyway? I don't even know."

"You don't *know?* Why don't you ask Sandy? Sandy *knows.*"

Now the children had heard their mother's name and all the crying started up again. "I mean before that. For God's sake, Nora, let it drop. He's a perfectly decent person."

"I'm not hearing this," Nora said. Then a thought of utter horror occurred to her. "Did you *walk home* with him?"

"No," I said. "Of course not. It was a heavy dinner and I felt like walking."

"He let you walk all the way from downtown alone?"

"Stop this. Stop. You two go home. I'm going to put the children to bed."

"You swear to me, Mother. Swear that you will never see that man again."

"He lives in Somerville. I'll see him at the grocery store."

"You know what I mean."

"Good night, Nora."

"Swear it. I am absolutely not leaving until you swear it."

For a second, a picture of that reality crossed my mind. Sandy and Tony and Sarah had already moved home; now I would have Alex and Nora as well. Everyone waiting in a line for the bathroom in the morning. Me in my bathrobe, ladling up six little bowls of oatmeal. "Sure," I said. "I swear it. Now go."

Alex was ready to go; this wasn't his fight. He leaned over and opened the door so that I wouldn't have to. For a tax attorney, Alex was a fairly regular guy. But then, he would have to be a steady sort to make it work with Nora. "Night, Mom," he said.

"Good night," I said. "Thanks."

Nora blew out like a storm. Not a word to me or the children. So I swore; what did it even mean? I wasn't going to see Romeo, anyway. I hadn't seen him in fifteen years and it would probably be another fifteen years before I saw him again. So what?

I put the children to bed, the last vestiges

of any happiness from my evening stomped out like a bug beneath my heel. I was sixty and back to buttoning up flannel jammies. But on that front I won't complain. They were sweet children, and even though I wished that Sandy's marriage had worked out and that they all lived in another house where they knew all sorts of happiness and stability, most days I didn't mind having them there.

"You're not going anywhere, are you?" Tony said, his voice all trembly. He was such a little boy for eight.

"Down the hall and straight to bed is the only place I'm going." I leaned over and kissed him hard on the forehead until he giggled and squirmed.

Sarah slept all the way through the putting on of the nightgown and the hoisting into bed. The crying had finished her off.

I kept my word to Tony and went straight to sleep. But I did have a dream that bears mention. Romeo Cacciamani was throwing pebbles at my window, something I've seen in the movies but have never heard of anyone doing in real life. I got up from my bed in the dark and pulled up the shade and opened the window to stick my head outside. In the dream my window opened easily, and there was no screen to contend with. In the dream I was wearing a very pretty white nightgown that was cotton and had been ironed.

"What do you want, Romeo Cacciamani?" I said.

He was standing in the middle of the street in his khaki pants and windbreaker, looking up at my window. I could see everything because the moon was so bright. He looked so handsome in the moonlight. How had I always missed that? I wanted to put my hand on his cheek. "What do you want?" I asked again because he wasn't saying anything. He was just staring.

"I had to see you," he said finally. "I couldn't sleep. I knew I was never going to go to sleep again if I didn't get to see you." He stared for a while longer, and when it seemed he was content, he smiled at me and waved. "Good night, Julie."

"Good night, Romeo."

And then I woke up. Here's the worrisome part: I was standing at the window. I've never been a sleepwalker and I wondered if this was something dangerous, if I could have fallen out. Then I remembered that the windows were all stuck and I never could have opened one without a hammer. I figured by the time I got the hammer I would have woken up, anyway. I looked out onto the dark night street. There was no one there. There was no one there and I was a nut. The dream made me feel embarrassed and a little bit sad to think that my subconscious could want such a thing. I went back to bed but never did go back to sleep.

In the morning Sandy came into my room without so much as a tap on the door. "You went out on a date with Romeo Cacciamani?"

"Absolutely not," I said. I had been lying in bed staring at the ceiling thinking about ordering carnations. "We ran into each other at this conference and had dinner. End of story."

Sandy closed the door behind her. It was six A.M. and the children weren't awake yet. Sandy was wearing sweatpants and a Celtics T-shirt with Larry Bird on the front. She had her glasses on, and the springs of her hair had yet to be brushed down. Her lip began to quiver. "Why would you do that to me?"

I sat up in bed, alarmed. "No, honey, not to you. This had nothing to do with you."

"Why else would you have dinner with him?"

"Sandy, I don't know. It was such a small thing. We ran into each other, we started talking, we got hungry, we ate. That was it. I promise you."

"You hate the Cacciamanis." She was wiping beneath her eyes with the back of her hand. She was so sensitive, poor Sandy. She didn't get over things very well.

"I did hate them, you're right. But when I saw Romeo yesterday I just didn't hate him anymore. A lot of time has passed, don't you think?"

"He's Romeo now?"

"That's his name."

She came over and slumped down on the corner of my bed. "Some things that happened never go away," Sandy said. She was too thin. Ever since her divorce, I could see her shoulder blades sticking out behind her like wings. "If he was around, if I had to hear his name, I really don't think I could stand it."

"He isn't around. He isn't here."

"So you won't see him anymore?"

"Do you have any idea why you hate him

so much? I'm just curious. Why do we hate those people so much?"

Sandy looked like I'd slapped her. "You don't even remember?"

"Of course I remember. I meant before that."

"What more reason do you need? I'm trying to get my life back together. I thought I was going to feel at home here."

"You are home."

"But you're going to keep seeing Mr. Cacciamani?"

"I'm not seeing Mr. Cacciamani. I just ran into him. One time in fifteen years."

Her face brightened a little. She wiped again beneath her glasses. "So you aren't going to see him again?"

"I have no intention of doing so."

"So you won't?"

These girls, they did not give me an inch. What difference did it make? It was an easy thing to promise. I wouldn't see him. "I won't."

Sandy got on her hands and knees and crawled up to me on the bed. She was thirty-two years old, but sometimes she reminded me of Sarah, who was very mature for four.

She put her arms around my neck and lay down beside me. "I really love you, Mom."

I told her the truth without explaining how extremely complicated that truth felt to me at the moment. I told her I loved her, too.

chapter four

When my girls were growing up I believed them to be the beating heart of the world, the very center of the universe. Unfortunately, they knew I believed this and so they came to believe it themselves. As far as they were concerned I was their mother, pure and simple. I thought it would be different after they were grown, but even when Sandy had children and Nora took on her huge career, they still never thought of me as the same sort of living organism that they were. They were in their thirties now, competent women in every way, but if we were all in the kitchen together, they would read the newspaper while I chopped the tomatoes for their salads. They painted their nails while I set the table. I knew I was to blame for this, something I had done had made them this way, but as far as I could tell, the horse was gone and shutting the barn door was nothing more than a gesture.

So they had made me promise and swear and do everything short of stick a needle in my eye to keep me from seeing Romeo again. They could not imagine that I wouldn't do what they wanted me to do, as that was the nature of our relationship. And maybe they were right. We were talking about Cacciamanis, after all. In life we are defined by what we hate as much as we are by what we love, and maybe it would be bad to give up all that definition. Maybe without the Cacciamanis to hate, the Rosemans would simply be unable to carry on. Maybe the hate was our skeletal system, the very thing that allowed us to walk upright, and without it we would be nothing more than a lump of skin and muscle on the floor. I could hate him again, I was sure of it, even though I had been thinking of him all morning in distinctly unhateful ways. Sixty years of hate versus one plate of decent spaghetti and a long walk? No contest.

Sandy had dropped out of college in the beginning of her junior year. She was bored with the work and happily in love with a fellow whose name was also Sandy. They married and became Sandy and Sandy Anderson, believing the novelty of a shared name would be enough to sustain their relationship. They were wrong. Now Sandy the husband lived in Maui, where he taught surfing, got stoned, and forgot to pay his child support, and Sandy the wife went to school three nights a week in hopes of becoming a licensed practical nurse. During the day she helped me out at the flower shop and I paid her a salary I could not afford in hopes of giving her a sense of independence. I was in all ways a flexible employer, and when she came in she was a good worker. She was charming to the customers and had a nice way with flowers. Her arrangements were pretty and cheerful, just like the kind my mother used to put together. (Mort's flowers, on the other hand, had aspired to look as much like the FTD promos as possible. They appeared to be two-dimensional even as they were sitting in front of you.) Sandy was also very good about deliveries. She never dawdled in the heat and she had a brilliant sense of direction, which she certainly did not inherit from me. The day after my dinner with Romeo, Sandy and I went in early to get the morning's deliveries ready and then packed them into my car, which had a more reliable engine than hers.

Sandy looked over the delivery sheet. "Well, at least everything is nice and close today. I shouldn't be gone long at all."

I told her to be careful. I always worried about her knocking on strange doors. I stood on the sidewalk and waved as she pulled away. In the days of my parents, and later under the administration of Mort, we had a white Ford van with the name ROSEMAN'S painted on the side along with a big bouquet of roses. I loved that van. It made me feel successful. But when times started getting tight, the van was the first thing to go. The insurance alone was eating me alive.

I liked being alone before the store opened, and I took my time sweeping up and wiping down the glass door. I moved the bucket of stargazer lilies out to the sidewalk. It was a cool day and we needed to sell them soon if they were going to have any petals left on them. I took out the little chalkboard and wrote *$10.00 a bunch.* Then I thought better of it, wiped the board off with my sleeve and marked them down to eight dollars.

The phone rang, some guy wanting to send an apology bouquet. "I've been bad," he told me.

"I understand." He said he wanted to spend seventy-five dollars, not including tax and delivery, so I figured he had been really bad. "What do you want to say on the card?"

The line was quiet for a while. "Don't know. What would you want to hear?"

"I don't know," I said. "You haven't done anything to me."

"But what do other guys say? I'm no good at this."

"The basics are usually safe: 'I love you.' 'I'm sorry.' "

"I like that. Write that down."

"And her name?"

"Catherine."

"Catherine with a *C* or a *K?*"

Again there was quiet. "No idea."

I sighed and wrote it out with a *K.* "If it's wrong, I'll tell her it was my fault."

"That's brilliant," the man said. "I only wish I could blame the rest of it on you, too." He gave me his credit-card number and I wrote it down.

I pinned Katherine's order to the cork-board and then went into the cooler and started changing the water and clipping back the stems so that everybody would get a better chance at life. For all the years I'd been in the store, I'd never gotten tired of the flowers. I'd gotten tired of the bills and the credit-card companies and the bad checks. I'd gotten tired of people who bring their bouquets back five days later for a re-fund because they died. But the flowers themselves still amazed me. I will always be moved by the sight of a hundred pots of hy-drangeas crowding the floor on Mother's Day weekend or the row upon row of trem-bling orchid corsages when the proms roll around. I was in the business of happiness. There were funerals, of course, hospital stays, but even then the role of the flowers was to cheer. Mostly it was about love. Flow-ers provide a means of expression for peo-ple who don't know what to say. Hand the person you love a bundle of flaming poppies, their twisted stems heading in every direc-tion, their petals waving out like windblown flags. They look so promising, so much like life. They'll get the message.

We weren't open yet, but I had unlocked the door to put the lilies outside. I was in the back, working my knife across a bunch of rose stems, when I heard the bell chime. I wiped my wet hands on my jeans and went out to the front. There was a time I would have sent whoever it was away, told them I wasn't open yet, but these were different times: If I'm in the store, I'm open.

There between a display of potted chrysanthemums and a bucket of terribly expensive freesias stood Romeo Cacciamani.

"You've got a real nice store," he said, checking out the inventory. "You know, I've never actually been in here before. My parents used to tell me the Rosemans sold voodoo stuff, dried bats, eye of newt. Do you have any eye of newt?"

What I thought: Why am I wearing this disgusting shirt of Mort's?

What I thought next: How long ago did Sandy leave?

What I said: No newts.

He nodded. "You've never been in Romeo's, have you?"

Romeo's was the name of his store, named for him by his parents, a tribute to their one and only child. It was a romantic name, of course, a flower-giving sort of name. It also drove my parents insane because they came before us in the phone book. At one point my father actually considered changing the name of our store to A. Roseman's.

"I've never darkened your door." I was so glad to see him you would have thought he was dropping off my lottery check. How could I be that glad?

He knelt down beside some sweet peas I had just gotten in and began to fluff them out a little. I was thankful he was focusing on the sweet peas, which were hard to come by, reasonably priced and dazzling in their freshness. If he had paid close attention to the stargazers, I would have killed myself. "I think you'd brighten the place up." He did not look in my direction at all, and it would have been reasonable to assume he was talking about the flowers.

"So maybe someday I'll see your store." What was he doing here, exactly? Out at the Mount Alburn cemetery, my father was doing loops in his grave. Cacciamani hands on our stalks. Besides, if Sandy was to walk in the door there would be a meltdown to rival anything in Chernobyl.

"Julie Roseman," he said to the flowers. He said my name exactly the way he had in the dream when he was standing underneath my window, and it caused my heart to stop for one beat and then start itself up again from memory. "I had a very nice time last night."

"I did, too," I said. "Until I got home."

Then he looked up at me. "You didn't tell them, did you?"

"I thought it was funny. I don't know what I was thinking. It was a huge mistake."

Romeo shook his head. "I told everybody I went to a movie by myself. I do that some-times."

"A movie. I wish I'd thought of that. How many do you have at home?"

"Well, there's me, and there's my mom. Plummy's living at home because I am barely making tuition at B.C., and room and board is just not a possibility. Then Alan, he's my youngest son, he's thirty-two, he got laid off last year. He had a really good computer job and then nothing, so now he's home with his wife, Theresa, and their three kids, Tommy and Patsy and Babe. They've got a dog, too. Junior. Do you count the dog?"

"I do."

"Okay, so there's nine of us. I've got a duplex, but it all gets mixed up as to who is living where."

"Well, you're making me feel better about my own life."

"One daughter, two kids." He shook his head. "You have privacy. I don't want to hear any complaints out of you."

"You were smart not to tell them. Privacy is having the good sense not to tell. But my God, dinner. You'd think we'd committed a crime."

"Remember how you felt when you found out Tony and Sandy had dinner?"

"Yeah, but they were kids. It's a little different." I looked at my watch. I didn't want to be rude, but even more than that, I didn't want to be caught. "Listen, I don't mean to rush you, but Sandy is going to be back here any minute and I'm just not up for a repeat performance. I know that's terrible. Everyone should be over this dreaded curse by now, but they aren't, so . . ." I shrugged. He was still down there with the sweet peas and I didn't know what else to say.

"So why did I come?"

"We might need to jump ahead to that point, yes."

"I had a really nice time at dinner last night."

"Really nice," I said. I could feel the sweat

coming up under my arms, and I swear to God it was the sweat of fear, Sandy looking for a parking space, Sandy locking the car.

"I haven't done this in such a long time. I was nineteen when Camille and I got married. Did you know that?"

I told him I did not.

"A guy gets out of practice."

And then, of course, I saw it. I'm not being coy when I say I was so out of practice myself that I couldn't even see the glacially slow lead-up to the question. Maybe in another setting, another time, I would have taken some pleasure from this. I would have strung it out and enjoyed it, but now I was only in a hurry. "Would you like to have dinner with me?"

He smiled a smile so grateful, so relieved, that I wished I had asked him the minute he'd walked in the door. He nodded his head.

"Good. When?"

"Tomorrow."

Curse fate and baby-sitting. "Can't happen," I said. "Sandy has school tomorrow and I've got the kids. Sandy, Sandy. You really need to get out of here."

"Tonight."

I would be lucky if I had time to get my hair washed tonight, and forget about buying a dress I couldn't afford. Still, he had seen me wearing jeans and Mort's old shirt, so his expectations couldn't be too high. "Tonight. Would you mind going out the back?"

"Fine," he said. He started to stand up and then reached for my hand. He had been squatting with those flowers a long time. I pulled him to his feet. For a second I held his warm hand. For one more second he covered my hand with his other hand. I felt a small current zip up my arm and go into my chest.

"I'll pick you up."

"No, no," he said with a certain panic in his voice. "Can't do that. What if we meet at the library?"

"My grandson likes to go to the library. He'd tell."

He closed his eyes. "Why can't I think?"

"The CVS in Porter Square," I said. "Seven o'clock."

And then I saw her, Sandy, through the window. "Out," I said, pointing to the back. "Go, go, go!"

For a sixty-year-old man whose legs were stiff, he managed to fly when he needed to.

Romeo Cacciamani was out the back in a flash and I, for the first time in thirty-nine years, had a date.

All day long I worked to keep my fingers free of the scissors' blades. I knew that I was bound to chop one off. I mixed up orders, filled in twenty-five-dollar arrangements with roses, and forgot to hand out a single packet of floral-life food for fresh cuts.

"What is it?" Sandy kept asking me. "Are you mad at me about this morning? Are you worried about Tony and Sarah?"

I assured her it had nothing to do with her, but Sandy could never have believed such a thing. "I'm just tired," I said. "I didn't sleep well."

Finally she relented. It was time to go and pick up Sarah from preschool. We weren't busy and so I told her to take the rest of the day off. I tried to sound magnanimous, but she'd probably planned on taking it, anyway. Once she was gone, I called my best friend, Gloria. Gloria had suffered mightily through her first marriage and had been rewarded in her second one. We had been friends since the seventh grade. She was my maid of honor and the person who drove me to my divorce hearing. Gloria and I go way back.

"Cacciamani!" she said. She was laughing so hard that she finally had to put the phone down and get herself a glass of water.

"I'm insane."

"You were insane for hating the guy all those years. You aren't insane for going out with him. I think he's nice. He's good-looking."

"You know him?"

"I don't *know* him, but I've bought flowers from him. I've talked to him—'Hello, how's the weather?' sort of thing."

This seemed inexplicable to me. "What were you doing buying flowers at Romeo's? I thought you bought your flowers at Roseman's."

"I always buy them at Roseman's now and I usually did before but, honey, I've got to tell you, Mort drove me insane. The man could not stop talking. If I was in a hurry, it was just so much easier to go to Romeo's."

"You have a point there. So you don't think I'm awful? The girls are going to hate me."

"The girls will never know if you have an ounce of discretion in you. You're an adult, after all. You deserve to go out. Besides, I never could figure out what in the hell this family feud was all about, anyway. Why did all of you hate them so much? I can remember when we were kids, your dad used to go on about the Cacciamanis so long I thought he was going to rupture an artery."

"That's the weird part. I don't know why we hated them. And Romeo doesn't know why they hated us. Just a tradition, I guess."

"So the tradition is over. What are you going to wear?" Gloria had more experience in the world of dating than I did, which is to say she had some in comparison to my none. "Where are you going?"

"We're meeting at the CVS in Porter Square."

"That pretty much leaves all of your options open, though I'd say nothing too fancy for a drugstore. Do you know what he likes to do?"

"He likes to walk."

"So flat shoes. We're not getting very far."

I sat down on a stool and rested my head against the corkboard. "Maybe I should call him, tell him just to forget it."

"Put perfume behind your knees. Men love that."

"I don't think he'll be coming in contact with the backs of my knees."

"What about birth control?" she said soberly.

I laughed. "Nonissue, thank you very much. Isn't it enough that I'm worrying about dinner? Do you have to make me worry about the things that aren't going to happen, anyway?"

"You're better off if you're prepared, emotionally speaking. You have to think through all of the scenarios."

But I couldn't think through any of them. Not even the one where I made it to the drugstore. Suddenly I was paralyzed with a kind of fear I hadn't known since Mort told me about Lila. "Listen, Gloria, be a best friend, will you? Come over tonight and pick me up. Show everybody that we're going out to dinner and then drive away with me. The girls will get suspicious if I go out again tonight."

"What am I? The beard? You want me to drive you to the drugstore?"

"If you could," I said. I was ashamed of how small and pathetic my voice sounded.

"Sure, Julie," she said. "I'll be your alibi any day."

I closed the shop a half hour early and

went home to go and sit in the tub. The house was miraculously empty and the quiet gave me a false sense of peace. Maybe it would be all right. Maybe we would have a nice dinner and nobody would find out. Gloria was right. This was not a crime. The only thing I disagreed with her about was the perfume. Florists never touch the stuff. We understood there were too many beautiful smelling things in the world to even try and compete.

chapter five

Sandy, Tony, and Sarah came back from McDonald's at six o'clock, the contents of their Happy Meal boxes still proving to be a great source of entertainment. At six-fifteen Nora walked in. I would have bet money on it.

"I was just showing a house down the street," she said, perfectly cool. "I thought I'd drop in and say hello." Nora had on an emerald green suit with an Hermès scarf tied loosely around her neck. My little Harley girl. She would have had a real future with the CIA.

"You look awfully nice," I said. Sandy, who was playing the role of the poor relation in her jeans and sweatshirt, looked like she had divided her day between plants and motherhood, which she had. She sulked off toward the kitchen, encouraging the children to sit in chairs while eating some ice cream.

"You look nice yourself," Nora said. "Going out?"

"I am, actually. Gloria and I are going to dinner."

"In the middle of the week?"

"We eat during the week."

"I was just wondering," Nora said.

"Well, don't."

"Maybe I'll stick around for a minute. I haven't seen Gloria in ages. She's happy with Buzz, isn't she?"

"Things turned out very well for them."

Nora paced around a little, smoothing down her skirt, readjusting a lamp shade. She didn't want to be there. She wanted to get home to Alex, but she still had to check up on me. I couldn't be too mad at her considering that her worst suspicions of my character were exactly correct and I planned to betray my promise to her in a CVS just as soon as I could get there.

"What was the house like?" I asked. I would have liked to have had the extra time to look at my lipstick, to wipe it off and reapply it a half a dozen times, which I remembered to be the classic predate ritual. I wanted time to be nervous instead of having to sit in my living room and make small talk with Nora.

"What house?"

"The house you were showing. Was it near here?"

Nora tilted her head slightly toward the east. "Over there."

"Sounds lovely," I said.

Nora sighed and threw herself into a recliner, forgetting all about the careful positioning of her skirt. "What about the shop? How are things going?"

"Not good—you know that."

"I don't see why you just don't give it up. Take the capital out and get yourself a condominium. Maybe something in Florida. You know that Alex and I will help you out."

"I want to make this work."

"It's not *going* to work, Mother. The business falls off every year. You've got to walk away while you still have some assets left in the place, otherwise the whole thing is going to be a bust. Everything Daddy worked for is going to be for nothing."

"It was never your father's work. It was my father's work." I had made a solemn vow to myself never to talk Mort down to the girls, but where business was concerned, I failed.

Mort had done a good job. He made the place thrive. But he never cared about flowers, and in the end he didn't care about me, either. I was in no mood to hear about how I was ruining his hard work.

"Call it whatever you want to call it," Nora said. "What I'm worried about is you. I want to see you come away with something. It's the Cacciamanis—you know that, don't you? That's the reason the business is failing. They poison our name in the community every chance they get. The big weddings, the fund-raising dinners, that business is all going to Cacciamanis."

"We do plenty of weddings. In fact, I've even been thinking about starting a little wedding planner business on the side. I'm always helping girls find a caterer and pick out their bridesmaids' dresses. I think it could be a great expansion."

"I think they're anti-Semitic." Nora never listened to me.

"That's crazy. Why would you say such a thing?"

"Oh," she said, looking absently toward the candy dish on the coffee table. "I'm out with people all the time. I hear things."

"You hear things from your father and they aren't true."

"You're sticking up for them."

"I'm not sticking up, but you can't call someone anti-Semitic just because they don't like you. Are we anti-Catholic?"

"Of course not."

"Well, what's the difference?"

Nora stood up and somehow managed to look down at me slightly even though I was taller than she was. "You just don't understand."

"Jesus," I said. Then the doorbell rang and I was awash with gratitude. "I'm going out to dinner. If you want to wait here for me, fine." I went into the kitchen and kissed Tony and Sarah good night. Sandy looked at me wistfully for a minute and so I leaned over and kissed her, too.

Nora had let Gloria in and they were standing in the living room laughing, the best of friends. "Time to go," I said.

"Maybe I could come," Nora said. "Alex has a meeting tonight and I don't have any plans. It could be fun, just the girls."

Gloria took a deep breath and put her hand on Nora's shoulder. "Honey," she said, "forgive me, but I need your mom all to myself tonight."

"Is everything okay?"

Gloria shrugged and managed to look both hopeless and brave. "I've just got some things I need to talk to her about. She's such an angel to me, you know. You're lucky to have such a wonderful mother."

"Hi, Gloria," Sandy called from the kitchen.

"Hi, sweetheart. Kiss the kids for me, we're running." Then Gloria put one arm around my shoulder and manhandled me out the door before any further discussion could evolve.

The night was crisp and clear, but there were never many stars to speak of in Somerville. We threw out too much light of our own and washed them away. I got into Gloria's Plymouth and she all but floored it getting off my street. "I thought you were just being a wimp wanting me to pick you up tonight, but that felt like a regular jailbreak."

"They're watching me."

"I should say so. I think we should drive around for a while just to make sure Nora isn't having us tailed. Do you know where she got those cute shoes?"

"I have no idea. I haven't even had enough time to be nervous."

"Well, you look good."

Gloria was the one who looked good. She had had her eyes done last year, and while I swore I had no interest in plastic surgery, I had to admit the results were impressive.

"I remember I used to tell my mother I was spending the night at your house in tenth grade when I was sneaking out with Jerry Shapiro. You were such a good cover. My mother always thought you were a wonderful influence on me."

"I was once a wonderful influence," I said.

"I'm just glad to be able to return the favor. You need to have a little more fun, Julie. You look pretty boxed in, if you ask me." Gloria pulled up in a red zone in front of the CVS. It was ten minutes until seven. "Do you need me to pick you up?"

I shook my head. "I'll get home fine."

"Or maybe you won't." She leaned over and gave me a kiss. "Think positive."

I wondered what I could have been think-ing of, asking a man to meet me in a store with fluorescent overhead lighting. Slowly, casually, I began to make my way up and down the aisles, trying not to look so incredibly suspicious that I would be arrested for shoplifting before he even got there. In the makeup aisle bottles of tan foundation claimed to make your skin young and dewy. There was a line of nail polish called Fetish. I picked up a tube of lipstick called French Kiss and then put it back in its plastic slot. Skin creams offered the miracles of youth, the overnight face-lift, and an age-recovery complex. The magazine aisle was not kinder. "What Your Mother Never Told You About Multiple Orgasms," "How to Make Him Beg for More," "Great Sex at 20, 30, and 40." I stopped and picked that one up. What happened to great sex at fifty? And what about sixty? Why was there no "Great Sex at 60"? Were we finished? Unentitled? Too thrilled to be taking our grandchildren to swim practice to even think about sex? Too awash in the fulfillment of our golden years to want a piece of the action? I put the magazine in the rack with its back cover facing out, a girl and a boy, all wet and sand smeared, running through the waves with their surfboards and cigarettes. It didn't make me feel any better.

By the time I had wandered over toward the pharmacy, I was ready to call it a night. Lubrication creams next to adult undergarments. A wall of condoms in every conceivable color and texture, all promising protection from sexually transmitted disease. I had forgotten about those. Lambskins and Magnums. Condoms that came packaged like the gold chocolate coins of my youth. The magazine was right. I was over, out of business. I was standing there staring at the boxes, reading the hideously depressing slogans ("For Feeling Like Love"), thinking that sex was a sport for the young, when I felt a tap on my shoulder.

"Shopping?" Romeo said.

I wasn't wearing my glasses and so my nose was approximately three inches away from a box of condoms. "I think this may be the single worst instant of my life," I said.

"Good," he said. "Then things can only go up from here."

Romeo smiled at me and I thought he must be right. He took my hand and led me out of the contraceptive aisle, which was considerate because if left to my own devices I would have simply tried to claw my way out through the floor.

"I was thinking we could go into Harvard Square and have sushi for dinner. Do you eat sushi?"

"Raw fish?"

"I know, I couldn't believe it, either. Plummy got me into it. It's what college kids eat. It's really good once you can get past the raw part, but if you don't want to do that, we can go someplace else."

"No," I said. "Given the circumstances, I would say raw fish is exactly what we should be eating. It's reckless food, don't you think?"

"I do."

As we left CVS and walked toward the car, Romeo kept holding my hand. It's a wonderful thing to have somebody hold your hand. Mort held my hand as we were walking back down the aisle after our wedding, but that was the last time. After that I held hands with my daughters when they were little, crossing the street and walking through parking lots until one day they got too big for it and pulled away from me. I missed that, the sweet and slightly clammy contact between us. I was glad to have Tony and Sarah to hold hands with again. I was gladder still to be holding hands with Romeo, especially since I knew he had picked mine up not because he was afraid I might dart out into traffic but because he liked the way my hand felt inside his own.

A piece of dating advice for the out of practice: If you're nervous about a date, especially if it is a date with your sworn enemy, try shaking off that nervousness by doing something that you would feel even more nervous about, say, skydiving, armed robbery, or eating sushi. The restaurant was pretty, very quiet, with paper walls and soft lighting. The music seemed to be a flute accompanied by a brook, and there was an ikebana arrangement at the hostess station that Romeo and I both admired. I let him order because not even the most enlightened feminist knows how to order sushi if she's never eaten it before. The waitress brought us a bottle of cold sake, but when I picked it up, Romeo took it away from me. "Never pour your own," Romeo said, filling my glass. "It's bad luck. Plummy told me that." Then he handed me the bottle and I filled his glass. "To the most beautiful florist in Somerville," he said.

"Don't sell yourself short." I touched my glass to his glass.

"No really," he said. "It's you. It is absolutely you."

I felt drunk after two sips and it had very little to do with the sake. Then a black lacquered tray arrived, covered in slabs of raw fish perched on top of tiny bricks of white rice. Some pieces of fish were tied down with little bands of seaweed as if they were so fresh there was a chance of them swimming off. Suddenly the thought of having to eat my dinner seemed so much more frightening than having a date that I didn't feel nervous around Romeo at all. To celebrate I popped a piece of salmon in my mouth. It wasn't bad. The eel I spit discreetly into my napkin, as I did the abalone, which was a little bit like biting into a human ear.

"I used to do that, too," Romeo said. "You get used to it."

"That one?" I said, pointing with one chopstick. "I'd get used to that?"

"Anything," he said. He stretched his arms across the table and for a second he touched my hands. Then he took his hands back again. "I still can't believe I'm having dinner with you."

"It's pretty unbelievable," I said, wanting his hands back.

"I have to tell you, you didn't bump into me by accident at that seminar."

"What?" I put one hand casually up on the table just in case he wanted it.

"I was walking through and I saw this woman, this beautiful woman. I only saw her for a second but, I don't know, I felt like I knew her."

I wasn't loving this story.

"So I circled back around so I could see the name tag, only you didn't see me."

"Me?"

"Then I came back a third time. I practically walked right into you."

"I hadn't seen you before."

"We talked for a minute and then you were gone." He snapped. "I completely lost my nerve. I thought, Well, that's it. But even though I had every intention of leaving, I found myself sitting out in the hall and waiting for you. Do you ever just have a feeling about something, you know you've got to do it no matter what?"

"Not until recently," I said. I picked up the bottle of sake and refilled Romeo's glass.

"I'd like it if we could get to know each other better. As people, you know, not just as Rosemans and Cacciamanis."

"I think that's a fine plan," I said. "So, tell me about your children." Children were always a big part of the story.

Romeo smiled and leaned back in his chair. He liked his children, I could tell. "Oh, let's see. Camille and I started early. Joe, the oldest, he's forty. He owns a trucking company and he's doing okay for himself. He's married and has three kids. Then there's Raymond, he's still single. He works with me in the shop. He's the one who'll take things over—he has a great touch with flowers. Nicky is in the Air Force, stationed over in Germany. He married a German girl about five years ago and now they have two kids. Then there's Tony." He sighed. "You remember old Tony. He's thirty-three now. How old is Sandy?"

"Thirty-two."

"Tony works for the World Health Organization. He's over in Ecuador giving out vaccinations."

"Did he ever get married?"

Romeo shook his head. "Nope. I have to tell you, I think I really screwed things up for Tony."

"How do you mean?"

"I think Tony was in love with Sandy, and

not just kid stuff. I don't think he ever got over all that."

I thought of poor Sandy at home with her kids and their Happy Meals, her nursing books and her homework. She never got over it herself.

"Anyway, Alan I told you about. He and Theresa are home with their three. And then there's my Plummy. She's twenty. It was such a wonderful thing for Camille to have a girl. She's a real treat."

"And a real surprise, it sounds like."

"Five boys, we thought we were all through with that. We thought we had the whole rhythm thing down, and then Plummy. But you'll never hear me complain about that one."

"And you named her Plummy?"

"No, no, we named her Patience because Camille said that's what it took to get a girl. The boys all called her Plummy. I don't even know who started it. They'd say, 'Isn't she just Plummy.' I think they picked it up from the Beatles. The boys were all crazy about her."

I liked the idea of all those children, of a house full to bursting all the time. All their friends, their boyfriends and girlfriends and then later their children. All of the flowers for all of their weddings. "It sounds nice."

"Camille made it nice. She was a wonderful mother. I think back on all the things she had to do. I didn't understand it until she was sick, until I had to start doing them myself. She protected me from a lot of things, you know. She took care of us."

We ate green tea ice cream for dessert and drank tea out of little cups. We talked about the flower business, who we ordered from, where we got the deals. We laid out every trade secret we had, both of us, and I learned more over dinner than I ever had from a seminar. I told him how I wanted to do a little wedding planning on the side. That was the thing I was really good at, big parties, organization. Romeo said he admired that. He said he was crummy at organization. Romeo had hired on too many members of his family, and while he said his product was good, he had a tendency toward disorder. He once missed an entire wedding—bridesmaids' bouquets, altar decorations, reception centerpieces, all of it. He had it marked down for the next week. I, on the other hand, after five years on my own, still didn't feel like I had a handle on what I was doing, and every month the revenues slipped. One thing that I discovered was that we were both going broke.

It wasn't exactly a lighthearted conversation we'd stumbled into, but still I felt like singing when we left the restaurant. Romeo said he would drive me home, or at least he would drive me to the end of my street and let me walk home from there. When we got to the end of my street, he pulled over and turned off the car. "No one ever told me Rosemans were such good company," Romeo said.

"When we're not selling the dried beaks of nightingales."

"When Camille died I thought, That's it. I'd known her since eighth grade. We were each other's family. I thought, There's never going to be enough time to get to know somebody like that again."

"Sure," I said. From a distance I could see my house. All the lights were off. My own family safe asleep.

"But the thing is, I do know you. That's how I felt yesterday. That's how I felt tonight. I've been hearing stories about the Rosemans since I was born. They weren't the right stories maybe—" He stopped and drummed his thumbs against the steering wheel.

"I know what you mean," I said. "In the end a Roseman and a Cacciamani are all the same thing."

"All the same thing," he said. He had a way of repeating what I said and I liked it. It made me feel like he was really listening. And then Romeo Cacciamani did something truly miraculous. He leaned over and he kissed me. It was just on my lower lip at first, and then my upper lip. Little kisses, and after each one he'd pull away from me like it was over, that was it, but then he would come back for more. He put his hands on my face and ran his thumbs beneath my eyes, then he kissed my eyelids, first right, then left, then my forehead, and then the part in my hair. I put my hands on the back of his neck and kissed his mouth, his neck. This was the part that no one told me while they discussed the evils of the Cacciamanis. No one said they were such good kissers. I was dreaming, sinking, swimming in a warm dark river of kissing, kissing hands and chins, every kiss soft. I could smell the soap on his skin and the fabric softener in his undershirt. I could smell his hair and taste his mouth, which still tasted like sake and rice. Oh, Romeo, this makes it all worthwhile, all those nights of working late and coming home alone, crying over the books and the roses that came in with brown spots on every petal, the worrying about Sandy and Nora and the children, the anger at Mort, the missing my parents, all of it lifted off of me and was washed back by the sea of tender kissing, maybe not forever but for now, and frankly, what else was there? I was lighter in that moment. I was my best self, loving and gentle and kind. It was so good to see that woman again, so good to hold another person in this way and be held. If a giant asteroid fell on us at that moment, parked in a car at the end of my block, the touch of Romeo Cacciamani's tongue against my teeth, mine would be counted as a happy life, a good life.

I kissed him again. I knew nothing about time, but after a time we decided it was late enough.

"Can I walk you down?" he said.

"Better not." I leaned forward and kissed him again.

"We'll manage this, right? We'll find a way to do this."

"I have every intention of it," I said. I put my hand on his hand and then let myself out of the car. I had walked all the way from Boston to Somerville. Tonight I felt like I could walk past my house and keep heading west. I could walk to Rochester, to Cleveland, to Fort Wayne, Indiana. I could walk all the way to Iowa and through Nebraska, over the Rockies until I got to Oregon, and even then I wouldn't stop if I didn't want to. I could go into the ocean, I could swim. I was that sure of myself tonight. I could go on forever.

chapter six

I went up the stairs to my room in the dark. I knew the way. My lips were puffy and I kept touching them with my fingers, my tongue. They still had the goods. They could still come through for me when I needed them. After such a period of neglect, what a thrill to find they still had all their spring intact, they were still capable lips. I found the lamp beside my bed and turned it on. I sat down on the edge of the bed, bounced a couple of times. If I had been twenty, I would have gone to bed with him. I would not have known how to get out of the car after kissing like that. After twenty minutes or so I would have gone straight for the buttons like a lemming goes for the sea. But now I was older, more sensible. Theoretically, I was supposed to believe in relationships, getting to know a person, enjoying the magic of the time. I was supposed to be grateful for what I got.

So why was I sitting there on top of my bedspread thinking I was going to jump out of my skin? Why did I want to go running down the street to see if I could catch up to his car? Oh, they were beautiful things, those kisses, every one a masterpiece, but here alone in a room with a bed I wanted to put my head through the wall, I was so eaten up by desire. Sex. I had not had sex in five years. No, let's be honest, it had been more than five years. It was more like five years plus the last four or five months when Mort was here and we didn't have any sex and I didn't much care because I didn't know he was going. And before that how long had it been? My fifties had more or less been a sexual wasteland. Those were good years that I blew, years I could have been burning down the house night after night had there been someone who wanted me, someone I wanted. So maybe tonight I had a chance and I decided what . . . to wait? Why? Because maybe five years and four months wasn't long enough to get the hang of celibacy? Because I wanted to be sure, to get to know him better? Who did I know better than a Cacciamani? Because I didn't want him to think I was that kind of woman? I was that kind of woman! Just give me half the chance. I wanted to be, I would be, but instead I got out of the car, programmed by the decade known as the 1950s. I fell facedown on the bed and bit at my pillow to keep from screaming. I could picture Sandy and Tony and Sarah running down the hallway to my room. "Mom! Grandma!" they would cry. "What's happened to you? What's wrong?" And what would I tell them? "Kids, tonight Grandma had the chance to make love with somebody she really, really liked. Liked more than she ever thought she was ever going to like anybody again, and she just walked away from it." Mothers are so proud of their daughters when they say no and so painfully disappointed in themselves when they say the same thing.

So now what was I supposed to do? Sleep was out of the question, and since

I only had one thing on my mind, I didn't think reading or television was going to cut it. I thought about calling Gloria, but she would never forgive me for waking her up to say I'd missed my chance to have sex, just as she would never forgive me for not calling if I had had sex.

There was the strangest noise outside. It sounded like hail, which was impossible considering I had just been outside and seen the clear moon. It sounded almost like little rocks hitting the side of the house. Then I realized it *was* little rocks hitting the side of the house. I looked out the window but I couldn't see anything, so I went back and turned out the light. There on the sidewalk outside my house stood Romeo Cacciamani.

I put my shoulder onto the window frame and tugged at the handles with both hands. Damn Mort, who said we didn't need to hire a professional painter! Damn Mort, who said he could do the windows himself! He probably knew this would happen. He knew that someday Romeo would come here at night and I'd never be able to get the damn thing open.

He'd painted me in! The veins were pushing out in my forearms and I felt a distinct, hot pain in my neck. I hoped he couldn't see the horrible face I was making as I strained against the stuck window and then beat on the edges with my palms until they stung. Helpless, trapped, I looked down at him and saw he was motioning something; he was saying something without making any noise.

Come down, he was saying.

I flew down the stairs. I took them like Tony, three at a time. I was out that door and back into the night and into his arms before I even knew I'd left the bedroom, back into the universe of kissing, except now we were kissing standing up, our arms so tightly around each other you would have thought we were in an airport and one of us was being shipped out for a particularly hopeless tour of duty. It had been what? Ten minutes? Fifteen? But I had felt the loss of him more than I can ever remember feeling anything.

"Come inside," I said. I kissed him, once and then again and again. "I can't believe you came back."

"Julie Roseman," he said. "I didn't know where to go." Stop, kiss. "I just kept driving around."

"Come inside." Kiss. I wanted to kiss his neck, my God, I wanted to kiss his neck, but that would have meant leaving his mouth and I didn't know how to do that.

"I can't come in, you know that."

The front door was wide open and the house was dark. For a minute passion had made me stupid, and I was not stupid. He was right. Not inside. "Your house?"

"No, no, no."

"A hotel. I have credit cards."

He stood back for a second. We were dizzy. "Really," he said. "You'd go to a hotel?"

"Isn't that why you came back?"

"I just had to see you again. I didn't want to get my hopes up." He kissed me, hard this time, the kind of kiss that makes it abundantly clear what the other person has on his mind. It was joy. "I know," he said. "My shop. There's a place in my shop."

I went and closed the front door quietly,

a small gesture considering all the bang-
ing I'd done on the window, then we took
off for his car. We kissed at every stoplight, every stop sign. Why did car manu-
facturers think bucket seats were a good
idea? What I wouldn't have given for a
good, old-fashioned bench seat then. I
think it was all part of the conspiracy de-
signed to slow down the sexual revolution.
When we were repressed, they gave us
bench seats in every model car, but once
we figured out how to use them, they
stuck a gearshift right in the middle of
everything. I put my hand inside his shirt
and touched the hair on his chest. I would
have been nervous, I would have shown
proper decorum, but five years and four
months makes a woman forget herself,
and I had forgotten everything.

I had driven past Romeo's shop before,
but it goes without saying that I had never
been inside. It was in another part of
Somerville, the part I liked to say was not
as nice, when in fact it was absolutely
fine. There was no trouble finding parking
at eleven o'clock at night. We kissed
madly in front of the store while he fum-

bled with the keys. There on the street he ran his hands over my breasts and down to my waist and then he tried the keys again. WHEREFORE ART THOU, ROMEO? the sign said, and beneath that the word CLOSED.

Inside it was dark, and in the dim shadows that the streetlight threw in from the window I could see it was mostly bare. All the flowers would be in the cooler. I couldn't tell if it was nice or not, but I imagined it was beautiful, the Ritz-Carlton a hundred times over. "I have a little place in the back," he said. "I sleep here sometimes when I have a really big job to get out. I like to work at night." He locked the door behind us and started to turn on the lights, but I told him not to, somebody passing by could see.

"Good thinking," he said. He took my hand and squeezed it, but we were both suddenly shy. While I think we could have done the whole thing pressed up against the door if we hadn't been able to get inside, this sudden privacy left us momentarily unsure of where to turn next.

"Show me around," I whispered. I didn't want to make a sound.

"With the lights off?" he whispered back.

"Why not? You know where everything is."

He held on to me. I wanted it to be this way. I wanted to slow things down, not for a couple of months or weeks or even days but just for a few minutes, just so I could revel in what it felt like to want someone so badly and know I was going to get him.

"The plants are over here, mums, azaleas, some little potted perennials, African violets. I got some very cute pots of miniature hyacinth this year."

"Do you sell a lot of azaleas?"

"They fly out."

"I always figured people bought those at nurseries."

He stopped and kissed me until my knees felt loose and I had to lean against him. Had I known that such kissing existed in the world, I would never have married Mort.

"And these, these are my pride. Wait, let me get the flashlight. Stand right here, don't move." He disappeared into the darkness and came back with a circle of light. It skimmed across a table of brightly colored, floppy little animals, but I knew for a fact that Beanie Babies were not his pride and joy. Then he shined it across a table of orchids. "Look at them," he said. "Aren't they something else?"

And they were, like flowers from a lusher, more ingenious planet. There were big ones, white and heavy as saucers of cream, little amethyst ones, tiny yellow spiders the size of thumbnails. "I never had the nerve to try orchids," I whispered.

"They aren't so hard. You just have to understand what they need. I think they are the most beautiful flowers."

"Show me the cooler," I said.

"Really?"

I took his hand, kissed his fingers. Romeo Cacciamani, whose name I was never allowed to say at the dinner table, I kiss your hands.

He pulled open the big steel door and we stepped inside. There was a dim automatic light. It was exactly like mine. It must have been made by the same company, the same year. It was Tuesday, so a shipment had just come in. There was just enough room for the two of us to stand. The flowers were packed in tight, bundles of twenty-four roses in plastic wrap, gerbera daisies and five kinds of lilies, pink and yellow stock, larkspur, Japanese iris, and buckets of leatherleaf ferns, jade, and galex. The flowers were up on shelves, they were everywhere. They surrounded us and pressed in against us. I loved the smell, too many smells to separate, blending and mixing, becoming one another. Everyone complains about carnations. They think carnations are low rent but they smell like heaven and they last forever. Give me carnations any day.

Then, up on the top shelf, I saw an arrangement. A beautiful arrangement.

"What is that?"

Romeo looked up. "It's for a birthday, first thing tomorrow morning."

"Who did it?"

"I did it. Who do you think does the flowers around here?"

"You made that?" I said, my voice so soft it was hardly my voice at all. "You did that yourself?"

"Sure."

"Oh my God," I said. "You really are a better florist than I am. That's brilliant. I mean it. That's one of the best-looking arrangements I've ever seen." It seemed reckless and at the same time had perfect balance. I never would have thought to use the tiny lilies of the valley and the foxgloves in with these giant white peonies. Almost white, they were a little pink around the edges with a few thin veins of red, and then there were white English roses, as big as the peonies. Where did he find roses like that? How did he dare to spend the money on them? White tulips came up from everywhere and all of it balanced, balanced like it was a painting, a perfectly composed still life, a carving in white-pink marble. But it was nothing like art. It was more like something that had simply occurred in nature and soon would grow and spread and take over the room. I had been looking at flowers for as long as I can remember using my eyes, and I had never seen anything so perfect before. "I think you may be a genius."

"What a nice thing to say." And when

he kissed me this time, we both knew we were ready. I wasn't nervous at all now. I was happy, so happy it was all I could do to keep from laughing. Where else should two florists come together than in a walk-in cooler stuffed to the rafters with flowers? It was cool, right at forty degrees, but that was a cool that I was plenty used to. He pulled my sweater up over my head and I unbuttoned his shirt, buried my face against his chest. Tomorrow I would walk into my own cooler and open up the packages of South American roses and it would never be the same. There was only a dim bulb in there, maybe forty watts. If there had been more time or more light I might have thought about my weight, my underwear, but maybe not. In that moment I was so happy with Romeo, I felt happy with myself. We took off our clothes and stood together naked and holding each other as much for warmth as for love.

"Julie, it's freezing. There's a bed in the back."

I nodded and we let ourselves out of the freezer. To all the magazines that only document sex up to forty, I say this: Have you ever walked naked with your lover through a florist's shop at midnight? No? Then don't tell me about sex.

The way was dark and he held my hand, stopping to kiss me and touch me. The very hands that had arranged those flowers arranged me now. We were Adam and Eve and this was a dark, flowered Eden. "In here," he said.

"Who's that?"

"Romeo?" I whispered. "Is that you?"

"Raymond?" said Romeo.

"Dad? Dad is that you?"

Maybe a better woman would have stuck by her man, but my reflexes were too good for that. I was flying naked through the store. The lights came on just as I leapt for the cooler door. If Raymond Cacciamani caught sight of my naked backside, I will never know. I pulled the door behind me tight and cursed the safety precautions that did not allow me to lock it from inside. Our clothes were all over the place, strung over dahlias, crushing down the baby's breath. I untangled them, his from mine, and inserted myself as quickly as any human being has ever

put on clothing. As for my beating passion, my heart's desire, forget about it. All
I wanted now was to exit.

There was a knock on the door. Romeo
was calling my name, wanting to know if
I was all right.

"Sure," I said. "Absolutely."

I was pretty much put together when
he came in wearing a ratty plaid bathrobe.
"That's my son, Raymond. He was working late. He fell asleep."

"Well, he's up now."

Romeo found his underwear and
stepped into them while keeping on his
robe. He dressed as quickly as possible,
but he had nothing on me. "We have to
go out there now."

"I'd rather not," I said. "I'm good with
coolers. I'm going to be fine in here."

"I have to take you home."

"I don't see how," I said, but I knew he
was right. I knew we were leaving. He
opened the door and took my hand and
together we came out of the cooler.

Raymond was standing there in his
boxer shorts and T-shirt, his arms folded
across his chest. He was bigger than his

father, softer in the face and with less hair, but still a nice enough looking guy. He had a big grin on, like this was a very funny moment, until he saw who I was.

"Raymond," Romeo said. "This is Julie Roseman."

"I know who that is," he said. "And she can get the hell out of this store."

"Raymond!" Romeo said. It was his parental voice. I had one myself. Even though the son was clearly in his late thirties, the tone had some effect on him.

"How could you bring, bring—" He was struggling to find a properly awful word. He did not succeed, thank God. *"Her* here."

"Mrs. Roseman and I are friends," Romeo said. I didn't blame him. There was no right thing to say.

"How you could bring her into Mama's shop. How you could bring her here. What is Grandma going to say, you bringing a Roseman here to fuck?"

"Raymond, stop it, I swear to God."

"I won't stop it," he said, his own voice raised now. "Not a Roseman. Not a Roseman in this store. Not a Roseman with my father."

I must confess this outburst had very little effect on me, except to increase my wonderment at what, exactly, had gone so wrong between us. This Raymond was not so different from my own girls. We could line our children up on either side of the room and they could scream at us until our ears bled.

"I'll take you home, Julie."

"She can walk," Raymond said.

At that point Romeo turned and went at him, I think went at him to strike, but Raymond held up his palms and stepped aside. "Forget it," he said, and turned to walk out of the room. But before he left, he did the most remarkable thing of all: He said my name, and then he spit.

chapter seven

"We are cooked," I said on the drive home. We had both been quiet for a while, both of us stunned as if by a sharp blow.

"Raymond," Romeo said, shaking his head. "If it had been Joe, all hell would have broken loose. If it had been Nicky or Alan, even Tony, I might have believed it. But Raymond is so easygoing. Of all my boys, I would have guessed that he would be the one who wouldn't care."

"We have such good luck," I said glumly. "Do you think he's going to tell?"

Romeo sighed. "I guess I better get back there and try and talk him out of it. Raymond I can deal with, but if they all get into this, it's going to be impossible." He pulled up in front of my house. Too much had happened for us to try to play it safe.

"Not to sound too much like a teenager,

but do you think I'm going to see you again?" I asked.

"You're going to see me. You're going to see me everywhere you go. I'm crazy about you, Julie Roseman."

I kissed him again. The last thing either of us was feeling right now was sexy, and yet I knew I was crazy for him, too. I said good night and for the second time that night I unlocked the door and went upstairs to my room.

I would have thought I'd spend the night staring at the wall and wringing my hands, but I don't think I'd ever been that tired in my life. I barely struggled out of my clothes, which I left in a heap on the floor and fell into bed.

When Sandy woke me it was bright outside, not just light but daytime. "I took the kids to school already. Are you feeling all right? Did you and Gloria tie one on last night?"

I really had to think about what she was talking about. I could barely open my eyes. Dear Sandy had brought me both a cup of coffee and an alibi. "I don't know what I was thinking of," I said, reaching for the coffee. "Gloria is such a bad influence on me."

"White wine?" Sandy asked.

"Manhattans," I whispered hoarsely. "Then pinot noir with dinner."

"Grape and grain," Sandy said sympathetically. "You shouldn't ever do that. Red wine always does me in."

"Tell me about it."

She patted my knee beneath the covers. "Well, I'll go on in and get things started at the shop. You come when you can. Do you think you can come in?"

"Oh, sure. I just need a minute to pull myself together. I'll be right behind you."

Sandy smiled at me, her heart full of sympathy for my hangover. She closed the door quietly behind her.

I leaned over and called Gloria.

"Naked?" she said. "You met his son naked?" Again, she was laughing to the point of blind hysteria. I thought about hanging up on her, but she was my only ally.

"Shut up," I said. "I mean it. I have no sense of humor this morning."

She sputtered a few times, laughed a little more, and then cleared her throat. "Okay," she said. "I've got this under control. I'm with you."

"I wasn't naked when I met him. I made it back to the cooler and put my clothes on."

"So let me get this straight: You had sex before you met the son or after?"

"Neither. We never got there."

"You went through all of this and you didn't even get any?"

"You have to believe me, after I met the son, sex was no longer on the agenda. I don't know if it's ever going to be on the agenda again. I feel like I could coast through another five years of celibacy after last night."

"He's going to tell, you know. You might as well get ready for it."

"Who? Romeo?"

"No, the son, Raymond. He'll tell all those little Cacciamanis. You're going to have some major repercussions from this, I'm afraid."

"Poor Romeo," I said.

"I'm not talking about Romeo. I'm talking about you. Those people hate the Rosemans, Julie. You watch your back."

Gloria read detective stories. She liked to

use phrases like "Watch your back." I told her I would.

After taking the most cursory of showers, I pulled on a T-shirt and some jeans, put a smock over that, and headed to the shop. At the stoplight I had a fashion moment and pulled my hair into a ponytail. I should have spent the day in bed with cucumber slices on my eyes, but I figured work was the only way to take my mind off my problems. I thought I would call my distributor and see about ordering some azaleas. I couldn't imagine where this thing was headed or how I would see Romeo again, but when the despair felt like it was going to strangle me, I would remember those kisses, in the car, in front of the house, by the orchids, in the cooler. Those kisses were my salvation. They threw a life raft into the sea in which I was drowning and pulled me up.

I parked the car and headed into the shop. Through the window I saw Sandy talking to a customer. Then I looked again. I knew Sandy's every expression, and even from a distance I could tell she was cowering. I heard a loud voice. I stepped up my pace considerably.

I thought at first that we were being robbed. That a man without a gun had come in in broad daylight to simply scream at Sandy until she handed over the till. I was ready to jump him. I was in that kind of mood. A fistfight would have been right up my alley this morning, and if things didn't go my way, well, I was feeling like a fatalist.

"Hey," I bellowed, slamming the door behind me. "What's going on here!"

Sandy slumped against the counter in relief, tears streaming down her face. "How could you?" she said to me, her voice breaking into sobs.

"How could I what?"

Then the man turned around. Who knew which Cacciamani he was, there were enough of them to fill a small town. Probably the military son had been flown in from Germany by some special envoy just to kill me. This one was bigger than Raymond. This one was huge. The seams of his T-shirt hardly seemed up to the task of holding the fabric together over so many muscles. He looked like the guy who played the killer in funny movies, the one who never speaks but bends iron bars into pretzels with his bare hands. Still, though, he had Romeo in his face, and I felt at once fear and a weird sort of fondness for him.

"So you're Mrs. Roseman?"

There was no sense splitting hairs on my title. I told him I was.

"I was just telling your daughter here what a tramp her mother was. I guess it runs in the family. She didn't catch my brother Tony, and you're not going to get your hands on my father or our business."

Sandy sank down into the little wicker chair we kept behind the counter, put her head down next to the cash register, and gave herself completely over to her grief.

"Look, Mr. Cacciamani," I said. "I would like nothing better than to set things straight between our families, but this isn't the way we're going to do it. Now, I need to ask you to leave my store."

He looked at me; maybe he looked a little puzzled or maybe I'm giving myself too much credit to think I could flummox him at all. "No, *you* look. You understand what I'm saying. I don't want any of you, *any of you,* coming near my family. I can make you very sorry, Mrs. Roseman. My grandparents, my parents, they kept their little feud going with insults, the cold shoulder, a little bit of screaming every now and then. That was fine for them, but you're dealing with a different generation of Cacciamani now, *capisce?*"

I opened the door. "Out."

He leaned back against the counter and folded his arms, which barely made it across his massive chest. "Not till I know you understand what I'm saying. I know you Rosemans aren't so quick."

Maybe I should have been afraid of him, but I just kept thinking, No way is Romeo's son going to slug me. This was all some ridiculous war that none of us understood, and it was up to me to not knuckle under to it. "Which son are you?"

He held up one finger to illustrate his rank. "Joe."

"Joe, you take your threats against me and my family and get out of my store, or so help me God, I'm calling the police."

"And tell them what? You're a slut?"

"Where does this language come from?" I said. How could someone who still hadn't had sex in over five years be a slut? No sense in trying to explain that one to him. "Out."

"It's okay," he said, straightening himself

to his impressive full height. "Maybe you do know what I'm talking about." There were five pots of tiny daffodils on the counter and he leaned over and pinched off all their heads and held them in his hand. While he was stripping my plants, he leaned over and said to Sandy, "Tony was never going to marry you. He told me you weren't any good."

She didn't even register it as far as I could tell. She kept her head down.

"Think about it, Mrs. Roseman," Joe said as he walked through my store dropping a careful trail of daffodil heads in front of him as he went, like a flower girl at a wedding. When he finally made it through the door, I locked up behind him.

"Christ, what a gorilla!" I felt it all coming back, I will admit it. The flame of hatred for all things Cacciamani shot up in my chest. I did my best to turn it down. Joe Cacciamani didn't understand, just as, until very recently, I had not understood. He probably wasn't such a bad guy. He just had a different way of dealing with people. He owned a trucking company. It was a different milieu.

I walked back behind the counter and started rubbing Sandy's back. Poor Sandy, it was a much bigger blow for her than it ever could be for me. "Sandy, are you all right, honey?"

"Don't touch me."

My hand stopped in mid-circle and I held it still. "Did something happen before I got here?"

She kept her head down. Her massive collection of tiny dark curls covered every bit of her face and shoulders, so that her head looked like a poodle sleeping on the desk. "He said you were chasing Mr. Cacciamani through his shop last night when his brother Raymond came in and made you stop. He said you were naked."

"Oh, Jesus."

Sandy flipped her head up. She wasn't wearing her glasses and her contacts had probably been washed away in a flood of tears. " 'Oh, we were drinking Manhattans last night, ' " she said in a high-pitched voice. " 'Gloria and I drank a whole bottle of pinot noir.' Did you actually make it all up in advance, Mother? Did you figure out what wine you would tell me you'd been drinking?"

"No."

"All I asked you was to not go out with

Mr. Cacciamani. I came to you first. I said, 'Mother, this would really be hard for me if you went out with him.' I thought you would understand. Everything"—she hiccupped and started to cry again—"everything about Tony, about that part of my life, that was really painful for me, and so I asked you please do not go out with him. It wasn't like I was asking so much. I mean, you always hated his guts after all, you always called him 'that greasy little Cacciamani weasel.' Would it be so much for me to ask you not to go out with the greasy little Cacciamani weasel? It's not like there aren't a couple billion single guys on the planet for you to choose from. You couldn't respect me that much? You had to just look me right in the face and lie to me? Poor, stupid Sandy, just tell her what she wants to hear and then go right ahead and do what you want to do. Is that the way it is for you, Mother?"

I looked at the little headless daffodil plants, their cheerful pink and blue tinfoil pot covers, their healthy green stalks pointing energetically to nowhere. I could see it both ways, her way and mine. Mothers don't like to hurt their children, not even when all they're doing is trying to have a life of their own. "Sandy, I am just so sorry I hurt you, and you're right, I never should have lied to you. But if you could see it from my perspective . . ."

"I don't want to."

"Well, give it a try, anyway. When you were in high school, you loved Tony and your dad and your grandparents and I all took it very personally. We thought you were trying to hurt us. We thought you said you loved him just to make us angry. But I know now that wasn't true. You didn't care that he was a Cacciamani. He was just Tony, the boy you loved. It just happened that way. You can call it a coincidence or bad luck or whatever you want. We were wrong to tell you not to see Tony anymore. I wish I'd had more respect for your choices, because you've got to understand that where you were fifteen years ago is where I am right now. It's not that I want to be with a Cacciamani. I'd like nothing better than to wake up tomorrow and find out he had a different last name. But it's not going to work that way. I really like Romeo. You should understand that better than anybody. They're good guys, at least some of them are good guys. I don't understand about all this hate, but I have to tell you, I'm ready for it to be over."

Sandy blew her nose on a piece of green floral tissue and took a deep breath. "That's pretty much what I said to you when I was in high school. And you know what you said to me, Mother? You said, 'Get over it.'" Sandy straightened up her shoulders and looked me dead in the eye. "Get over it," she said.

chapter eight

Sandy took the rest of the day off which was to say she picked up her purse and walked out of the store, tears streaming, hair springing along behind her. How had I come to this in such a short time? I tried to retrace the events in my mind: a conference, a simple cup of coffee, would you like to take a walk? Yes, a walk, how lovely. I couldn't understand where I had ventured down the path to war crimes. But things were bad and I could only guess that they'd get worse. I thought about Romeo. I wondered if he knew by now that Joe had come to see me. I couldn't call him for fear of who might pick up the phone (would they recognize my voice—so soon?), and no doubt he was feeling the same way about calling me. The simple thing to do would be to knuckle under. It wasn't as if I knew this man so well. How much would it be asking really for me to just give him up? But I didn't want to give him up, and not just because I'm stubborn, which I am. The principle of the thing was reason enough to hang on, but it wasn't my reason. It was Romeo. How could I even say such a thing? Did I even know him? I knew him. He was right; we had been enemies for so long that we had bonded together. All the passion of hate had become the passion of love. The ions that had bound us together from the start had simply reconfigured. They were the same in number, the same in strength, it was just that they now played a soft samba in my heart instead of a Wagnerian opera.

All day long I went through my responsibilities in the dullest way. I handled the flowers as if they were pencils or spatulas. Every arrangement I put together I tore apart again, remembering the perfect bouquet in Romeo's cooler. I cleaned up every mess I made but I left the little headless daffodils in their place, even though all my customers remarked on them, touching the dried-out tips with their fingers. "These didn't do very well," they said sadly.

"No," I said, as if I hadn't noticed. "I guess not."

I kept waiting for the other Cacciamani boys to come harass me. I thought it would be like a fairy tale. Each one who came would be bigger than the last, their threats would be scarier, until finally some fire-breathing Cacciamani boy nine feet tall and covered in hair would break down the door frame as he entered my shop. "Release my father!" he would shout, and his fiery breath would singe off my eyebrows. But even under such duress I would continue to hold my ground.

"Sorry," I'd say to the fire-breather. "No can do."

And when that happened, when I had stood up to the very worst of them, the spell would be broken. They would all be restored to regular guys, decent sons who would dance the lambada at our wedding. It would be explained to me then: We were all victims of some ancient curse having to do with a slight made to some witch two thousand years ago in Bimini, something terribly far away from us for which we could not possibly be held responsible. My daughters would love Romeo and I would love his sons. The phone rang and suddenly my heart was filled with hope.

"I'm waiting for you at your house," Nora said. Then she hung up.

So the path to broken curses was going to be a little more treacherous than I had imagined. I flipped over the CLOSED sign and went to meet my fate.

I loved Nora, I know I have mentioned this before, but the sight of that Lexus in my driveway struck greater fear into my heart than the sight of Joe Cacciamani decapitating miniature daffodils ever could. I thought about that great old song, "You Always Hurt the One You Love," and thought that the inverse was also true, The One You Love Always Hurts You.

"Alex and I have talked it over and I've told Sandy that she and the kids can come and live with us," Nora said before I had both feet inside the door.

This before, Hello, Mother. This before, Heard you had a rough day.

"Nora, Christ, ease up on me, will you?"

"No, Mother, I will not 'ease up on you.' "

Where these girls picked up this irritating predilection for mimicking, I do not know. It was not a habit of Mort's or mine.

"When you look me in the eye and you swear something, I expect I can take you at your word," Nora said, her tone a subtle blend of hurt and righteous condemnation. "What can we count on now, hmm? Can you tell me that? What else are you lying about?"

"Okay, you win. You were adopted." This conversation was taking place in the entry hall. I was wearing my smock. My purse was in one hand, my keys were in the other. "Where are the kids?"

"Sandy thought it would be better if they didn't see you just now."

"Why, because I'm such an evil influence? I had a *date,* Nora, remember those? I don't really, because I haven't had one in thirty-nine years. A sixty-year-old woman goes on a date and the children have to be evacuated from the house?"

"This *date,* as you call it, isn't the issue, though you have a hell of a definition of a date, from what I hear. The issue is—"

"Hang on to that thought for one second, sweetheart, your mother needs a glass of wine in the biggest way." I dropped my keys into my purse and dropped my purse onto the floor. Then I headed for the kitchen. Nora followed close behind in her smart gray pantsuit. She'd been doing a lot of yoga along with her running and she was now impossibly fit, as supple and lean as a grey-hound. I wanted to tell her I couldn't argue with her while I was wearing dirt-covered jeans, not when she was dressed like that. It put me at a terrible disadvantage.

"The issue is trust," she continued. "The issue is honesty. The issue is *family.* The Rosemans do not keep company with the Cacciamanis. That was your guiding princi-ple when we were growing up."

I took the wine out of the refrigerator and held it up to her. She shook her head and so I poured for one. "I Made A Mistake," I said. "Tell me if I can make this point more clearly. I'm sorry. No one knows what we did to them or what they did to us. What hap-pened with your sister in high school could have happened to anybody, with anybody. Your sister is thirty-two years old now. It's time to put that one behind us."

"I can't believe I'm hearing this."

"Believe it."

"So you're telling me you're going to see him again?"

I took a sip. For a minute there I really wanted to talk to her, to open up and tell her about the jam I was in. She was my daughter, after all. Why did we always tense our backs before we spoke to each other? "I don't know. I'd like to. I'm just not sure if these are insurmountable odds. I've got you and Sandy to contend with, I've got his kids to contend with."

"Sandy told me she was afraid this afternoon. She thinks he might really try to hurt us. I'm calling the police and filing a report, I can tell you that much."

"You can't," I said. "You weren't even there." I took a longer sip. I took a drink. "I keep thinking this all might blow over and I could go out with Romeo. He's so nice, Nora. That's the thing you won't believe. He's the nicest man I've ever met." I had tried talking to her one way, now I was banking on compassion. Never bank on compassion where Nora is concerned.

"So that's your answer," she said. "I'm taking the kids."

"For what *reason?*"

"If you don't see it by now, I can't explain it to you."

"Well, are they coming back tonight?" For all the times I'd wished that Sandy would pull her life together and get a place of her own, suddenly the thought of them leaving seemed so awful to me. No little Tony to do homework with? No Sarah wanting me to put her hair into pin curls? I was a good grandmother. Maybe I was proving myself to be a lousy mother, but I was one hell of a good grandmother.

"Sure," Nora said, looking at her watch. "They'll be back in a few minutes."

"And then they're going to your house? Sandy has school tonight. You're going to take the kids?"

"Not tonight," Nora said. "I have to show a new listing and Alex has a meeting. In fact, I need to get going."

"So let me understand this, you're moving Sandy and the kids out because I'm an unfit influence, but you're doing it at a time that is more convenient to you?"

Nora started to say something, but then she thought it over for a second, raised her eyebrows, and nodded. "More or less."

"I won't hold my breath."

"Think about what I said, Mother." Nora was back in her yellow silk coat and sailing toward the door.

"Oh, I think about everything you say. I can't stop thinking about it."

After Nora left I had about ten minutes to finish off my wine and stare vacantly at the wall in the kitchen, in which time I came up with the idea of painting everything pale yellow. Then Sandy and the kids came home. For whatever my girls had been plotting, they seemed at least to have had the decency not to tell the children about it. Tony and Sarah came flying at me like I had just come home from a tour in the Peace Corps.

"We didn't see you last night and then we didn't see you this morning," Tony said breathlessly. "We haven't seen you in ages."

"Ages," I said, kissing his head madly and then his sister's head as well.

"Mom said you were sleeping in this morning. I said I wanted to sleep in like Grandma, but she says, Nope, up, you have to go to school."

"She was absolutely right." I looked over at Sandy, who was hanging back by the door. She had a guilty look on her face for having sicced Nora on me. No matter how mad she was at me, I think she realized the punishment did not fit the crime.

"I drew you a picture," Sarah said. "Because you were gone for such a long time." She knelt down and extracted a drawing from her tiny pink Cinderella backpack. It was a stick figure with her hair in a flip, and she was holding a giant bunch of flowers. The flowers went from the floor to past her head.

"It's divine," I said.

"It's you," Tony said.

After Sandy went to school, I shifted into total indulgence mode. I made popcorn balls with Karo syrup and played Go Fish with real enthusiasm (it's not *that* one plays Go Fish, it's *how* one plays Go Fish). We watched the video of *Lady and the Tramp,* a movie that I must say moved me almost to tears in my present circumstances. I identified with both Lady and Tramp. Since it was Friday, I extended bedtime by a full hour. In short, we partied. Maybe I was trying to secure my place in their hearts, but really I think that had already been done. I wasn't going to risk my family. I wasn't going to be bossed and I wasn't going to be foolish. The trick was finding the line between those two things. I tucked everyone tightly into bed, read every book that was requested of me, and made a series of exhausted good nights. I believe I was asleep myself no more than seven minutes later.

* * *

It was still dark when I felt a hand shaking my shoulder. I used to get up on my own.

"Grandma?"

I rolled over. "Tony, baby, what is it?"

"Somebody's stealing your roses."

I looked at the clock. It was five forty-five in the morning. "Are you having a bad dream?"

He shook his head and hustled himself under the covers. "It isn't a dream. It's a lady. There's a really old lady outside and she's stealing the roses."

Tony's bedroom was in the front of the house, just above the roses. "What does she look like?" I asked cautiously.

"A witch."

I was up and in my bathrobe in a heartbeat, a fluffy pink chenille number that Mort bought me for my birthday on a year I had hoped for something romantic.

"Don't go down there," he cried. "She'll do something awful."

"Not a chance, baby. I know who it is. It's a friend of mine. She's just going to borrow the roses. I just want to go down and say hello to her."

"It's too early."

"You're absolutely right. I thought she was

coming later. You sleep in my bed and I'll come up in just a minute and we'll sleep in together."

Again, I was running down the stairs, running through the door and into the yard. I had forgotten my slippers and the grass was cold and wet with dew between my toes.

The old bat had attached my hose to my spigot, something I had yet to do this season, and was watering the roses. It was too early for blooms, but they had their leaves already and some nice little buds. I could see it all there, a spade, two empty, giant-size boxes of kosher salt. She had to use kosher.

"Hey," I said. "Turn my goddamn hose off!"

She looked good for almost ninety, still tall and thin with a bunch of steel-wool hair. She was a little stooped, but then she had been digging. She looked at me with utter contempt, like I was coming into her yard instead of the other way around. "What are you doing up so early?" she said. "Rosemans are a lazy bunch, everybody knows that."

I ripped the hose out of her hand and

threw it back into the boxwoods still running. I didn't care how old she was, I was going to take her out. "Get away from my flowers. Get away from my family." Since my yard, like all Somerville yards, was about the size of a half bath, I was very much in her face.

"No, *you* get away from *my* family, you tart." She took her bony finger and she poked it into a soft spot beneath my collarbone in a way that actually hurt quite a bit. You could tell she had poked a lot of people in this exact spot in her lifetime and she knew just where to aim. There was a blue Dodge idling in front of my house and when the old bat poked me, out flies yet another Cacciamani boy, this one not quite as big as the other two, which ruined my theory of the expanding sons.

"Hey, you," he said, raising his voice to wake every neighbor who had dared to sleep with their window open on a cool spring night. "You get your hands off my grandmother!"

Old woman Cacciamani smiled and folded her arms, her rottweiler boy bounding up on me.

"Do you have eyes?" I said. "Do you see who is poking who here?"

"Whom," the old woman said. "Who is poking whom." She turned to Wolf Boy. "It's appalling. They can't even speak."

"Please," I said. "Both of you, stay exactly where you are. Make yourselves comfortable on my lawn. This time I am calling the police."

"Everybody in town knows you're a crummy florist," the old woman said. "You probably think salt is fertilizer."

"Shouldn't you be dead already?" I asked.

"Hey," Cacciamani Boy said, lunging again.

She raised up the skeleton of her hand, which was draped in a layer of parchment paper so thin it let through the first rays of morning light. "Alan," she said. "Wait for me in the car."

"I'm not leaving you alone with her. It isn't safe."

"Alan. The car."

What a short leash these men lived on. He turned in miserable obedience and slunk back toward the Dodge. He didn't get inside but leaned up against it, the muffler making a racket while going nowhere.

"I've had it with you Rosemans," she hissed. "I'm an old woman and I've lived to protect my family from the likes of you, your parents, and your whorish little girls. I will not leave this earth until I know that my people are safe from yours."

"For the remark about my daughters alone I should break your sorry neck, and I could, do not think otherwise. I am in a bad mood, Mrs. Cacciamani. You are pushing me too far."

"Come near my Romeo again and you'll know all about broken necks."

I tried to control myself. This could be my big chance after all, my shot at the truth. "Since you have ruined my sleep, frightened my grandson, and killed my roses, will you at least do me the courtesy of explaining to me what the hell your problem is?"

"You are unfit to be in the same room with my son."

"Fascinating. I mean before that."

"Your daughter tried to trap my Tony into a life of misery."

"Well, Tony surely contributed to that one."

"If he was going to marry her, it's because

she lied to him. She probably told him she was pregnant. She probably tricked him."

"Please," I said, breathing deeply. "Before I am forced as a mother to cut your heart out, I want you to think back before the business with Sandy and Tony. Use the last few brain cells you have and try to think. What went on between you and my parents? I know this didn't start in the previous generation because your crowd and my crowd did not run together in the Old Country." My hands were shaking. Every fiber of my being wanted to grab her and throw her to the ground and jump up and down on her chest. An old woman! Where was my decency? I have never felt such seething hatred in my life.

"Why should I tell you?"

"Because this is madness! It's insanity." For the sake of my neighbors I tried to control my voice.

She looked at me for a while. I hated to make eye contact; death seemed to be leaking off of her. "I owe you nothing." She went to poke again, but I saw it coming this time and I stepped aside, at which point she fell face forward into my lawn.

I backed toward my door, my hands

raised as a clear sign that I had not touched her and would not touch her. Cacciamani Alan came running back and scooped the old pile of sticks up in his arms. I turned my back on the family drama, utterly disinterested as to whether she was dead or alive. I went inside and closed the door.

chapter nine

I opened Sandy's door. She was asleep in a cloud of curls. "Get up right now," I said without much tenderness. "I need your help."

She sat up quickly. She was a mother. She was used to waking up in a hurry. "What is it?"

"The roses," I said. "We've got to move fast."

Nora would have rolled over and gone back to sleep, but Sandy knew by the tone of my voice that I wasn't kidding around. This was a higher priority than whatever argument we were having. I went to the linen closet and got a stack of sheets and towels. I went to the kitchen and got a box of twenty-gallon lawn and leaf bags. I went to the garage and got two shovels. I was moving. There wasn't much time. I didn't know if there was any time at all.

"What is it?" Sandy said, scurrying behind me. She slept in her sweats, so she was essentially dressed. All she had added were her glasses and her scuffs. I was still in my bathrobe. To hell with it.

"That old Cacciamani bitch salted my roses!" When I threw open the front door I half expected the paramedics to be there performing CPR on what was left of her. I imagined the yard would be taped off as a crime scene, but in the first pleasant surprise I've had in I do not know when, I found that all the Cacciamanis were gone, swept away in the blue Dodge. The only trace that they had been there at all were the two empty boxes of salt. She had taken the spade, so I guessed she wasn't terminal.

"She salted the roses?" Sandy said, stopping to stare at me in utter horror. "That's what Sherman did after he burned down the South. That's like the lowest thing one human being can do to another."

"Sherman salted the roses?" I stuck my

shovel in and heard a crunch. Sandy grabbed the other one and we were digging.

"He didn't just salt the roses. He salted everything. He wanted to ruin all the farmland so the people who came back after the fire wouldn't be able to feed themselves."

Sandy had done very well in history. She had a long memory for facts. "Yeah, well, I think she was operating under a similar impulse." I spread a sheet over the lawn. "Put all the dirt here. It all has to come up. We might have a chance, but it's going to be tough. She took the time to water it in."

"She *watered* the salt?" Now Sandy was really throwing her back into the digging. She wasn't hurt anymore. She wasn't scared. She was mad. She was my girl. "Only a total sociopath would stop to water the salt."

"That's not all," I told her. "It turns out she salted my mother's roses, too. Years ago. We didn't know it, of course. We just knew they died and nothing could ever be planted in that spot again." One good thing was the old woman wasn't strong enough to dig very deeply. There were still full pockets of coarse kosher salt in the ground, little rocklike diamonds shining in the black dirt. You had to kind of admire her for doing it herself, for making Alan stay in the car while she marched up my walk like Sherman to repeat the crime she had committed God only knows how many times before.

"How did your mother find out who did it?"

"She never did. Romeo told me." I pulled up the plants and gently loosened the dirt from their root systems, then wrapped them each in a towel. My Queen Elizabeth, my London Best, my Pink Lady.

"You think about this, Mother. You think about the kind of family who would do this."

I thought about it. Eight mature rose-bushes wrapped in towels on my lawn. I thought about it while I dug an even deeper hole beneath where the bushes had been to get out any salt that might have trickled down deep. The ground was heavy and wet and I felt like I was digging

a grave. It gave me some perverse satis-
faction to think of it as the old lady's
grave. "I'm thinking about it, Sandy. I'm
thinking about very little else."

When we felt we had dug wide enough
and deep enough to ensure clear margins,
we went to the garage and began lugging
out fifty-pound bags of dirt and fertilizer.
As a florist I get incredible deals on these
things; distributors sometimes give them
to me as an incentive. We loaded up the
ground with the best dirt money could
buy. Then I rinsed off the roses' roots in
the street just for good measure and together Sandy and I planted them all back
again. By the time it was over we were
mud-caked, exhausted, and proud. The
children, tired out from their night of fun,
were still asleep. Sandy came to me and
hugged me for a long time.

"She didn't win," I said.

"The grocery store is full of salt," Sandy
said.

"Then I'll dig them up as many times
as I have to."

"What are you going to do, Mother?"
Sandy said. We sat down together on the

front porch, too tired to make it inside.
"Really, what are you going to do?"

"I don't know yet."

"I've been thinking about what you said. I want to try and see it your way."

"I appreciate that."

Sandy looked down the street in both directions, maybe to see if we were really alone, if there wasn't another one lurking in the hedge. "Did Mr. Cacciamani say anything about Tony?" she asked tentatively.

Maybe this would hurt her, maybe it wouldn't. I didn't know anymore. All I was sure of was that I shouldn't lie to Sandy about anything. "He never got married. He's in Ecuador giving out vaccines." I reached over and took her filthy hand in mine. "Romeo said he was so sorry about what he had done to break you up. He said that Tony had really loved you, that he never got over you."

Sandy kept her head down for a minute, and I didn't know if this was going to start her crying again. "I know this is terrible of me," she said finally. "But I think that's the nicest thing that anyone has ever said."

Saturdays were always a juggling act. The store tended to be packed for the first half of the day and utterly dead after two o'clock. Usually we just brought Tony and Sarah with us, and if one of them had a party or a play date (I could not believe the social calendar these children had; Sandy actually had to write all their engagements down to avoid double-booking), then one of us would drive them over and hurry back to work. I liked having the kids in the store. It's like taking children to restaurants or on planes or anyplace else where other people are loath to see them. If you do it right from the start and make it part of their normal lives, they were usually very well behaved. Certainly I had grown up in this flower shop, and I knew that sitting in a corner for hours wrapping florist tape around wire gave me no end of pleasure. Tony liked to work in the back. The more tasks you gave him, the happier he was. While he was perfectly willing to sweep the floors and unpack boxes of ribbon, nothing gave him a sense of purpose like filling up stik-piks, which he accomplished to absolute perfection. What he wanted to do was strip the thorns off of roses, but I was twelve before my father let me have a knife. Sarah, on the other hand, was an up-front girl. She reveled in speaking to strangers. I believe that "May I help you?" was her first complete sentence. People were very charmed. That kid could have sold water to fish. When there were no customers around, she would check all the plants for dead leaves. She pinched them off gently, carefully, and stuck them in her pockets.

The four of us worked briskly. Sandy and I were both invigorated by our morning's triumph over the salt and our own tenuous reconnection. People loved to ask us questions about working together: "Is that your mother?" "Is this your daughter?" "Three generations? How wonderful!" This morning we all beamed our answers. "Yes, she is!" "Oh, she's pretty incredible, all right." "I'm very proud of her, yes."

But even in the midst of all the good feelings, I could not help noticing the man who was parked in an older black Ford across the street. He would sit there for a while and then drive away for an hour. When I thought he was gone for good, I would look up and there he would be again, sitting in his car reading. From time to time he got out and walked up and down the street a ways, but he never got out of sight of the shop. He'd stretch up on his toes and roll his shoulders, then he'd feed a couple quarters into the meter and get back in his car for more reading. Then he drove away again, then he came back. He was a heavy man in a black raincoat with a full head of close cropped silver hair. He looked Italian.

Sandy didn't see him. I know that for sure because if she had, she would have called the police. After days of threatening to call the police myself, I knew there was no point in doing it now. As much as I knew that man was there for me, I couldn't bring myself to call and complain about someone who was parking, parking with an unexpired meter. As the shoppers came in and the traffic picked up, car after car would pull up behind him and turn their blinker on, waiting for him to pull out. But the man in black just stuck his arm out the window and waved them around.

At two o'clock it was as if some unseen switch had been flipped and the customers simply stopped coming in. I can't explain it, but it worked that way every week. Sandy rounded up the kids to go home. I would stay until five, cleaning up whatever Tony hadn't gotten around to and working on the books. People like to know you're open until five on Saturday, even if they never come by.

"Okay," Sandy said. "We're off." She kissed my cheek in celebration of our good day together. Kissing was something we rarely did anymore. I held on to her for a second. I didn't know what was coming, but I knew it might be bad. I had a maudlin flash that maybe this was the last time I was going to get to see everybody. I hugged the kids. I could sacrifice myself to save them.

"Go," I said, trying not to choke up. "Have a fantastic day."

I stood at the door and waved good-bye to them. Tony and Sarah loved to wave and be waved to. After they had gone I just stood there at the door. It was nice of him to wait until my family was gone. It made me feel better, knowing it was just me they wanted.

He watched Sandy and the kids drive away and then he tossed his magazine on the seat beside him, got out of the car, checked the meter again, and came across the street. I was sick with dread but wanted to appear brave. I held the door open for him.

"My," he said, "that's service."

He was dressed as a priest. I hadn't noticed the white collar before. I was sure he caused less suspicion that way. "What do you want?" I said straight out.

He looked at me a little puzzled. "Want? Oh yes, some flowers. I was thinking about getting something different for the altar. We're in a bit of a rut."

I sighed. All the work of my day fell on me all of a sudden, the digging, the sales.

I felt old. "Cut the flowers," I said, not intending any pun. "Just get to it. I'm really tired of you people. If you're going to shoot me, shoot me, whatever."

Now the man looked very puzzled. There was not one chance in the world that he was a priest who had spent the entire day in his car trying to figure out what floral arrangement he wanted for his church. "Shoot you?"

"Whatever your plan is. I don't know. Threaten me, scare me to death—whatever it is you have to do, I just want to get it done, okay?"

"Do you know me?" the man in black asked.

"Sure, you're the guy who's been parked across the street off and on since nine o'clock this morning, waiting for my daughter and my grandchildren to leave so that you could come in and have a private word with me. Am I right so far?"

"Oh, I am bad at this," he said, looking genuinely crestfallen. "It never occurred to me that you might notice."

"And what you have to say to me has to do with the Cacciamanis, correct?"

"How do you know all this? This is very impressive. Romeo was right, you really are something. Except for the shooting part. You're wrong about that. I have no intention of shooting you."

"Romeo?"

"I'm Father Alphonse," he said, sticking out his meaty hand. "You can call me Al."

"Father Al?"

"Just Al is fine. Whatever you feel comfortable with. You're Jewish, right?"

I nodded.

"It's all about what works for you. I answer to anything. I'm not so crazy about Alphonse, but you can call me that if you want."

"Romeo sent you?"

"It isn't really part of my job description: baptisms, weddings, last rites, courier service. It could be a new direction for the church to go in, though." He chuckled at his own joke. I might have chuckled, too, at another time, but as for now I was completely beyond jokes.

"And Romeo sent you because . . ." I was trying to prompt him.

"Well, he's stuck. He can't call you, he can't come by. He's being watched by his family, you're being watched by your family. The idea is that no one suspects a priest, which is funny because you did suspect a priest. You really do break all the rules."

"I've been told that."

"Romeo and I go way back. All the way back. From first grade at St. Catherine's. He was lining up for the priesthood himself, you know. Did he tell you that? Then he met Camille on a bus. He made the right choice. She was a great woman, Camille." He gave me a nervous look. "Meaning no disrespect to you."

"None taken."

"When God took Camille, Romeo never thought there was going to be anyone else for him. He thought his life was over. And he kept on thinking that pretty much until he met you."

"Me?"

"Romeo is crazy about you," the priest said.

Crazy about me? I wanted to kiss him for that. What a yo-yo this was. Hate Cacciamanis, love Romeo. Hate Cacciamanis, love Romeo. "Nobody else in his family is crazy about me."

"Have they been giving you a bad time?"

"I wouldn't know where to start."

Al shook his head and clucked his tongue. "Romeo was afraid of that. He's very worried about you. He wanted to come here, but he thought that might just make everything harder."

"He has good instincts."

"There's a lot of bad blood between your families, a great deal of pain."

I looked at him. He had a pleasant face, dark round eyes and a wide mouth. "Say, you wouldn't happen to know what's behind all this, would you? You're a priest, people tell you things. Do you know why our families hate each other so much?"

"People do tell me things, but I'm not allowed to repeat them."

"Not even in emergencies?"

"Sorry." He took an envelope out of his

coat pocket and handed it to me. "I can give you this, though."

The envelope said *Julie* on it. I wish I could say my heart leapt at the sight of Romeo's handwriting, but I had never seen his handwriting before.

"Go ahead," he said, "read it. I'm supposed to wait for a reply." Al turned his back and stared at the asters. He leaned over to sniff them. I opened the note.

Dear Julie,
I told you when I met you again that I had been wanting to write you a letter. Well, here it is. Sorry doesn't begin to express how terrible I feel about everything that has happened. If you are in half the trouble that I'm in, then you know what I'm talking about. As much as I know the answer is to walk away from each other and forget about it, I just can't do that. Please meet me tomorrow morning in the CVS at nine o'clock. Tell Al I'll go to Mass tonight. Give me one day so that we can, at the very least, make things right between us, even if we

can't make things right between our families.
Love,
Romeo

"Oh," I said, holding on to the paper.

"Good news, I hope," Al said.

"I don't know," I said. "I don't know what constitutes good news anymore."

"Well, you don't have to give me an answer now." He took out his wallet and gave me a card. There was his name, his number, and the address at St. Catherine's Church. It would have been like anybody else's business card, except for the little picture of an upside-down dove on it. "You can call me. I have an answering machine." He tapped the card. "That's my private number."

I turned the card around and around in my fingers, trying to figure it all out. "Listen," I said. "If you're not in such a hurry, could you stick around for a little while? I know you've already been here all day, but if you could give me a little bit more time, say, ten minutes?"

"Sure," he said. "I've got ten minutes."

I put the letter and the card in the pocket of my smock. "Come in the back with me. I'll make you an arrangement. You said you wanted something new for the altar?"

"Oh, I was just making small talk. Romeo gives us our flowers."

"Well, this week I'm giving you the flowers. This week the flowers at St. Catherine's are brought to you by Roseman's. That will be a first, Jewish flowers."

"Flowers are flowers," he said. "I'd never turn them down."

I got Al a stool and he came and sat with me while I worked. The new flowers came in on Monday morning and so I gave him everything I had. If someone had come in asking for a bouquet I would have had to send them away, told them I was empty. It took me a lot longer than ten minutes, but I gave him my masterpiece. The flowers were graceful, towering. They reached the tips of their petals straight up to a Catholic God. It was not as good as Romeo's, but it was a deeply ambitious arrangement. It was all Al could do to work it into his car. He held my hand. He could not thank me enough.

"No," I said. "Thank you."

"Anything else?" Al asked me at the curb.

"Yes," I said. "Tell him yes."

chapter ten

I closed up early. Why not? There were no more flowers. I called Gloria.

"I need to shop," I said. "And I need advice."

"My two favorite things in the world. Can I give you advice while we shop?"

"That would be best."

"Buzz drove up the Cape this morning to fish. According to my calculations, he is absolutely stuck in traffic on Route Six about now. I'll pick you up."

Over the years I had wondered many times why my marriage to Mort couldn't have been more like my friendship with Gloria. Not that I needed Mort to go shopping with me (though once or twice in the course of thirty-four years would have been nice), but I wished I could have called him when I needed advice and thought he might be willing to drop everything. Gloria, I knew, would fly back from her first European vacation if I had needed her help, and I would have done the same for her. It was an understanding between us. Mort would tell me to hold on, whatever it was could wait while he puttered through the tasks at hand. When he did show up, he never would have remembered that I had needed something from him. When I asked him again, he would tell me to hang on one second and then he would go to get a sandwich. And even when I had his attention, it would wander away from me. "Julie, look at that," he would say as I was pouring out my heart. "Do you see that water stain on the ceiling? How long has that been there?" What happened was that over the years I just stopped asking, I stopped trying to confide. If I had a problem, I went to Gloria. If I had a little success that merited celebration, she was the one I called. If it was a failure, a fear, a questionable lump that required someone sitting with me in the doctor's office for three hours, it was Gloria, not Mort, who was there. Gloria, I knew, would love me unconditionally, as we had loved each other when we were fourteen and there was no one else to love. She told me the truth when I asked for it and

sometimes when I didn't. When we disagreed (rarely), we did so with respect. She
had seen me through Nora's biker phase and
Sandy's would-be childhood marriage. I had
seen her through her daughter Kate's ano-
rexia and her son Jeff's arrest after a one-
night spree of stealing radios out of cars.
After all our kids were grown, she stayed
with me and Mort for two months when she
finally left Shelly, her first husband. Mort
liked Gloria, but he groused, not about her
presence in the guest room, but about our
closeness.

"You're always talking," he said. "My God,
it never stops. You would think she'd been
in Tibet for twenty years instead of eight
blocks away."

But what Mort didn't understand was that
I wanted to talk. I wanted someone to hash
things out with, somebody who paid attention and remembered. That was Gloria. That
was not my husband.

I told her about old woman Cacciamani
on our way to Saks. I told her about Al the
priest as we pulled into the lot. When we
had secured a good parking space and
turned off the engine, I showed her the letter.

"You were holding out on me," she said,

digging through her purse for her glasses. I handed her mine. "This should have been first." She read it carefully and then she read it again. She held it up to the light as if to make sure it wasn't counterfeit. "This is good. And you said yes?"

"I said yes."

"I never would have thought otherwise. I wouldn't have a fool for a best friend."

"I have some decisions to make."

"He doesn't give you a lot of help with the dress code. And this business of always meeting at CVS is a little weird."

"It's only the second time. And the first time was my idea."

"That's fair enough. Maybe it will turn out to be 'your place.' You can go there for anniversaries."

We got out of the car and walked toward the store. I had no business spending money on anything, but after the last couple of days I'll admit I felt like I deserved a treat. "Help me control myself."

"How do you mean that?"

"Financially."

"That part is no problem. For the rest you're on your own."

We swung through the doors and immediately I felt comforted by the smell of perfume and face powder and new shoes. I always thought about Holly Golightly saying that nothing bad could happen to a person in Tiffany's. As far as I was concerned, the same held true for Saks.

Gloria stopped at the Chanel counter, politely brushed off the salesgirl, and ran three different stripes of lipstick across the top of her hand. "Now, the first thing you want my advice on is your clothes. That's the easy part. The second thing you want my advice on is Sandy and Nora." She rolled her hand back and forth in the light trying to decide which was her best color.

I picked up a tube called Splendor and drew a line across the inside of my wrist, making myself look like a victim of a suicide attempt. "Precisely."

"I want to tell you to lie. Every instinct I have thinks that you should lie, you know that."

"I do."

"But you won't, because you really can't. You lied once and it ended up so badly. Lying to your children is totally different from lying to your husband or even your friends. Lying to your children can have all sorts of psy-

chological repercussions for everyone involved, and you just don't want to get into
that.

"On the other hand." She stopped and
picked up a pretty black compact containing
four round pats of eye shadow, butter and
lavender, pink and gray. "Isn't this beautiful?
Don't you want to buy this? I never could
make any sense out of eye shadow." She
put it down and picked up her train of
thought. "On the other hand, telling them is
just going to be hell."

"Think Saigon in 1972."

"Right," she said. "That's your problem in
a nutshell."

"And the answer?"

Gloria smiled at me sadly. "There isn't an
answer, angel, because there isn't a question. You know you're going to tell them, you
know it's going to be awful, and that's really
all there is to it." Her eyes teared up a little
bit. Gloria was every bit as willing to cry for
me as she was for herself.

I felt comforted by the depth of her sympathy. The thing about talking to Gloria was
that it was a little like talking to myself, only
much better. With Mort I was always trying
to convince, to state and prove my case.

Gloria believed me right from the start. She only wanted to help me come to my own logical conclusions.

"So I guess that's solved," I said heavily.

"Well, at least that leaves us the fun part. Don't forget you're going to spend the day with Romeo tomorrow."

"I do forget that. Given how this day started out, it still seems pretty hard to believe."

Gloria discouraged me from buying the cotton sweater that came down almost to my knees. She encouraged me to buy a matching underwear set in a color the gorgeous twenty-something salesgirl called champagne.

"It's good with your skin tone," the salesgirl said.

"Black is too aggressive for the first time," Gloria said. "Black says you knew all along you were going to have sex."

"I don't know that we are," I said.

"See, all the more reason to go champagne."

There was lace on both the bra and panties, but not so much that I felt like I was trying to pass myself off as Belgian. "I'm so out of practice. I've been buying my underwear at Target for so long, I didn't know they sold it anywhere else."

"Welcome back to the world," the sales-girl said, and took my credit card.

Since I had spent all of my discretionary income on two articles of underwear, I decided to content myself with something I already owned for outerwear. Gloria thought it was a good plan, seeing as how he had never seen ninety-eight percent of my clothes, anyway.

She looked at her watch and steered me toward a phone in the women's lounge. "You need to call Nora now and tell her to come over."

"I can call her once I get home."

Gloria handed me a quarter and a dime. "Tell her you're on your way and you want to meet her there." She looked at me hard. "Do you want me to dial?"

I took the change and called my oldest daughter, who, to my complete surprise and disappointment, answered the phone. I requested the meeting.

"This is Cacciamani business, isn't it?"

"It is."

Nora sighed. "Sandy's already told me about salting the roses."

One positive side effect of all of this was it seemed to be bringing Sandy and Nora closer together. "Well, there's more."

"So much more you can't tell me over the phone?"

"It would just be a lot easier if I could talk to you both together."

Nora sighed again. Really, she had perfected the art of the sigh. It was at once bored and inconvenienced. "All right. I'll be there in a half an hour."

I hung up the phone and looked at my watch. "She said a half an hour. We're going to have to really move it to be there on time."

"You have to stop being so afraid of her," Gloria said.

"Why?" I said. "She's scary."

Gloria drove me back to the flower shop so I could pick up my car. "You're going to have a wonderful time tomorrow," she said. "We'll look back on all of this someday and have one hell of a laugh. It will be years from now, but it will happen."

I put my arms around her neck. "I'm going to have to take your word on it."

She tapped the horn twice and waved as she drove away. I wished that she could have come home with me, but she didn't

offer because she knew it wasn't right and
I knew it wasn't right and neither one of us
had to say it.

Dreaded Lexus. Enough of that. Sandy
and Nora were sitting in the kitchen. They
had plugged the kids into reruns of *Gilligan's
Island,* which I felt sure was doing them absolutely no good and very possibly some
harm, but we needed the privacy.

"So," Nora said. She was dressed casually, which meant slim black pants and a fit-
ted black sweater, with her hair pulled back
in a gold barrette. Sandy was dressed casually, too, which meant the Celtics T-shirt had
just come out of the dryer.

"So here's the thing." I sat down across
from them in the *Meet the Press* configura-
tion these family meetings usually took on.
"A priest came to see me at the shop today,
a Father Al, and he brought me a letter from
Romeo."

"After I left?" Sandy asked.

"Actually, yes. You had just gone."

"You're getting letters from Catholic
priests now?" Nora said incredulously.

"He didn't write the letter, he only delivered it, and you might want to pace yourself

because there's more to come." I couldn't help but think about the night I had called both of the girls home to tell them Mort had left with Lila. Sandy was married to Sandy Anderson then and both girls brought their husbands. It was so humiliating to have to announce my private life like that, to tell them all that my marriage had failed and that their father preferred a much younger, much more attractive woman to me. Both girls cried. They had counted on us always being together. I thought that night was the hardest thing I was ever going to have to do. It turns out I was mistaken.

"He wants to see you," Sandy said.

Bless her for that. "Tomorrow morning."

Nora looked at her watch. "Well, seeing as how it's seven o'clock now, I don't think you're calling us over so we can discuss this. I think you've said yes and you're just filling us in on the details."

"I wasn't planning on asking permission, if that's what you mean."

"The answer is no," Nora said, standing up. "We've been threatened and harassed, property has been damaged." Nora took anything concerning property very seriously. "These aren't just people we don't like any-

more. These are dangerous people. Dangerous to you and me and Sandy, not to mention the children. You just can't keep thinking
that you're the only person in this world
whose needs matter. You have to think about
your family."

I was trying to remember how Nora had
taken the news of her father's departure. I
wondered if she'd ever called him and
roughed him up, tried to make things turn
out the way she wanted. I had no idea.

"I'll admit things have gotten out of hand,
but I want to see Romeo again, I need to. I
just don't want to lie to you. You asked me
to tell you the truth, this is the truth."

Sandy was thinking about it. She was
holding the past in one hand and the present
in the other and making her silent assess-
ments. I asked her where she stood on all
of this.

"I think these are really, really crazy people," she said quietly. "And I think you're
making a mistake."

I could live with that.

"Don't call me," Nora said. "I have to de-
tach myself from this." She picked up her
purse and said good night to her sister, her
niece, and her nephew.

"Does that mean 'Don't call me and let me know how it goes' or does that mean 'Don't ever call me again'?"

"I'll let you know," Nora said, and then she was gone.

I had a real lump in my throat. It wasn't that I needed her approval. It wasn't that I was worried she'd never come back. But we had been having the same old fight for so many years that it just made me sad beyond measure. She was my daughter, she had been my baby. We had shared a body for a while. It seemed like ever since then I'd been missing her.

"So you aren't going to walk?" I said, turning around to Sandy.

"I'm not moving out, if that's what you mean, but I want you to listen to me, Mom. I think this is a serious mistake you're making. That's what you told me, and maybe for my age, for that time in my life, you were right."

I was fairly stunned by her admission. I reached out and petted her hair. "I'm just so much older." I felt so much older.

"I know," she said without any unkindness. "That's why you should know better."

Tony came into the kitchen with a flashlight. "Come outside, Grandma. I made you a surprise."

"He's been working on this all afternoon," Sandy said.

I followed my grandson out into the yard. He was holding a piece of paper in one hand and shining his flashlight with the other. He took me over to the roses, which looked perfectly healthy in their new bed of black soil.

"I know that woman wasn't coming to borrow the roses. I know she wanted to steal them," he said.

"Okay," I said. "You're right."

"So I did this thing. We learned this in Cub Scouts. See, I broke some sticks and set them in the ground, see?" He shined his light down, and sure enough, there were about a half a dozen small sticks set casually among the rosebushes. "Then I made a map that shows where all the sticks are now. Then every morning I bring out the map and I check to see if the sticks are in the same place. Mr. Hollins says you have to remember that the wind can blow them around some, so not to get upset if they aren't in exactly the same place, but you'll know if someone was there."

I crouched down and studied his work.

Tony was a seriously meticulous kid. "It's a good plan," I said. "Thank you."

"At least it keeps us safe," he said.

Let me extend the fairy tale, if I may. It was more complicated than it had originally appeared. It wasn't just the five frightening fire-breathing sons I would have to contend with. There was also a desert to cross and then a jungle of thorns. There were seven years of drought and then seven years of flood, followed by famine and pestilence and war. In addition there was a burden of doubt that had to be dragged behind me in a burlap sack at all times. It was absolutely written in the decree of my fate that Doubt had to come along. It had a whining, high-pitched voice that rang in my ears for every step I took.

"Are you sure?" Doubt would say. "Do you know him? Could he be worth all of this suffering you've brought on the world?"

"Shut up," I say to the sack.

"Have you thought of the people you love?" Doubt says. "The people you're hurting?"

"Shut up," I say.

"He may not even be there—did you think

of that? After all this time, it could all turn out to be nothing more than an elaborate hoax and you will be forced to live with the shame and embarrassment for the rest of your days."

"Shut up. Shut up. Shut up."

chapter eleven

I was up at six, up meaning out of bed. I had been awake since three. I conditioned my hair and blew it dry. I used some of Sandy's face scrub, just in case he decided to look too closely at my pores. I cut all the tags off my champagne underwear and put it on. It was pretty. It would have been much prettier on the girl who sold it to me, but it would have been too big for her, and anyway, she wasn't here. I changed clothes three times and then drew a line with myself. The next thing I put on was what I was wearing, otherwise everything in my closet was going to wind up on the floor and I was going to fall into the morass. I didn't know that this part of human nature survived. I thought that it had slipped away at some undefined age, like baby teeth and menstruation. I thought that I had outgrown the ability to look into a full closet and think that there was nothing there. Now here I was, living proof that it is possible to become a teenaged girl again. Finally I chose a pair of heavy linen pants and a dark blue boat-neck sweater, an outfit that I thought made me look smart but unconcerned. I was growing less concerned by the minute. All of the things I should have been worried about were falling away: There went Nora's wrath. There went all the Cacciamani boys' threats. There went the old matriarch, who may or may not have died on my lawn yesterday. The hardest thing to put aside was Sandy, but I'll tell you, I did that, too. I was happy. I was a woman getting dressed for a date with a man I didn't really know but who I knew I was crazy about. I put on the little amber drop earrings that I always got the most compliments on. I put on lipstick, wiped it off on a Kleenex, put on lip gloss. I slipped on my most sensible walking shoes.

Sandy was in the kitchen with a cup of coffee reading the front page of the paper. "You look so nice," she said. She looked mostly tired herself, like she might have been sitting there all night.

"I really appreciate that."

"Don't," she said. "Frankly, I'd rather you

didn't look nice. You know, I thought about nailing your bedroom door shut, but then I figured the hammer might wake you up."

"I always was a light sleeper." I poured myself a cup of coffee.

"I just decided there comes a point in every woman's life when she has to accept the fact that her mother is all grown up and she should be allowed to make her own mistakes."

"Are we there already?" I sat down beside her. "It seems like only yesterday I was holding your head back and trying to pour liquid penicillin down your throat because you were half dying of something but you didn't like the taste of the medicine."

She smiled a little. "I don't remember that. I mean, I remember the scene, but in my version I'm pouring it down little Tony. It's a sort of bubble-gum pink, right?"

I nodded.

"Maybe that's why this whole thing is harder for Nora. She hasn't had kids of her own yet. She hasn't been thrown up on so many times that there's no point in trying to look good anymore. She isn't used to being bent to somebody else's will. When you have kids you bend, you just have to. Kids make you good at not getting your own way anymore. I don't like what you're doing, but at least I understand that there's nothing I can do about it."

"Thanks, honey."

"Do you want me to drive you over there?"

I shook my head. "It's not far. I'm going to walk. It's nice outside."

"You and your walking. Mother, you are a constant surprise to me."

I shifted in my chair and stared at the clock. "It isn't time to go yet."

"Here," Sandy said, shoving half the Sunday paper toward me. It was as thick as a brick. "I'm going to make waffles for the kids. Do you want waffles?"

"No waffles," I said, picturing myself becoming sticky and having to change again. I spread open the paper. I went through all of it while the kids watched cartoons and jumped around with the energy that comes from Sunday morning syrup. I read Sarah the funny papers and Tony sat and listened to save himself the trouble of having to read them himself. I put on an apron and washed the dishes. Then I went into the pantry and alphabetized all the spices in the spice rack. That's what I had come to.

I looked at the clock again. "I could go now."

"If you want to be absurdly early."

"Where you going?" Sarah said. She tried to put her sticky fingers in my hair but I was too fast for her.

"Grandma's got a play date," Sandy said. She looked at me with some fondness. "Get out of here."

I kissed them each good-bye and made my break for the door. It was too early, but I couldn't control myself. I stopped off at the rosebushes and, to the best of my memory, Tony's sticks were all in proper alignment. The plants themselves seemed to have survived their trauma unscathed. If anything, with all that new dirt and fertilizer they would probably have a record-breaking summer. Then I started walking. I was only thinking about Romeo now, how much I used to hate him and how much I didn't hate him anymore. I was thinking about his hair, which was rough as a brush, half black and half gray. By the time I got to the end of Cedar and turned on to Elm, I was repeating his letter again and again in my mind. *Love, Romeo.* I was walking faster. When I got to the parking lot of the CVS, I was trying hard not to run. It was eight-thirty when I got there and I had a light sweat on my forehead. I went in the store (thankfully open twenty-four hours) and went straight to the condom section, where lo and behold, a full half hour early, Romeo was waiting.

We stood there for a minute, grinning stupidly at our own good fortune.

"You met Al," he said.

"A great guy."

"He really liked you. He said you thought he was going to shoot you."

"I'd had a bad couple of days."

"You are so beautiful."

"I was just thinking the same thing about you."

He reached out his hand and took my hand. I stepped toward him and then he kissed me. Very few people were in CVS at eight-thirty on a Sunday morning. There in the condom aisle I wrapped my arms around his neck and he crossed his fine hands behind my back. That kiss was worth everything. Even if every rose had died, that kiss would have made it right. It was tender and passionate. I tapped my teeth against his teeth. We bit each other's lips kindly. I used the muscle of my tongue for something better than conversation. We must have made a sight, two sixty-year-old people looking like they might just drop down on the flat-pile orange carpet and do it there in the birth-control aisle.

"Okay," he said. "Okay." He kissed my chin. "We've got a big day ahead of us." He took my hand and we started to walk out of the store. "Wait a minute." He stopped. "I want to buy you something."

"What?"

"I don't know, a present. Something from CVS. I mean, I think we should support the place. It's been so good to us."

I thought about it for a minute. "Licorice. Black licorice."

He nodded solemnly. "For you, two packages."

We went back to the candy aisle, dazed by the bright assortment, the shiny possibilities of sweetness. I decided on a package of Switzer and one of Nibs. Then we went outside and got into his car. He held the door open for me. You would have thought we were in the South.

"So, where are we going?"

"Surprise," he said. "Are you hungry?"

The thought of food was impossible at the moment. I shook my head.

"Me neither." Romeo was a good driver. "So, you met my mother, too. You know everybody."

I looked out the window and watched Somerville shooting past me. All of the McDonald's and Pay-Less Shoes, the endless stream of Dunkin' Donuts, they looked brighter to me now. Forgive me my sentimentality. It was suddenly a better-looking town. "I didn't kill her, did I?"

"She's fine. Just a little scratched."

"She poked me once. Then the second time I dodged it. I swear to God, I never touched her."

"She poked you?"

"She did, see?" I pulled down the neck of my sweater to show him the round purple bruise up high on the left side of my chest, showing also the strap of the champagne bra for good measure.

He looked while driving. "The Cacciamani stigmata!" he said. "You've been initiated. I've had that exact same bruise for probably fifty percent of my life. She has it perfected. She doesn't even have to look anymore and she hits right in the soft spot between the bones. It hurts like hell. None of us are ever smart enough to duck. We just stand there and take it. Boy, she must have been really surprised."

"It was hard to tell," I said. "She was going down. You've got a tough mother, if you don't mind my saying."

"I have a tough mother," he said with gravity. "She was a good mother in a lot of ways. She worked so hard for the business, she took good care of me and my dad. I think about what it must have been like for her, a pretty girl coming over from Italy all by herself, not speaking a word of English, but she just took it on. I don't think anything ever stopped her. But I'll tell you, she rules. I think she wanted to have a ton of kids and it was too bad she wound up with just me."

"That's not so bad, just you."

"She really was too much mother for one person," he said cryptically. "So, then when I married Camille and we had so many kids, she was in heaven. We bought the duplex underneath my parents' place—how's that for genius? I don't know how Camille even stood it. My mother just took over everything she touched. It was like my kids had two mothers, one who was really sweet to them and one who kicked their butts into line."

"She poked your kids?"

"She poked the kids. She poked my father. She poked the dogs. She even poked the mailman once for being late. He tried to sue her." He laughed a little. "I always thought it would stop someday. She's pretty old, you know, I thought she was going to be winding down. Now she's poking you." He shook his head. "I really am sorry about that."

"I'm sure if my daughter Nora had seen you, she would have done more than poke. How much trouble are your kids giving you?"

"I have to tell you, it's been a real surprise to me. There was a time the whole Cacciamani-Roseman thing was of great interest to me, but I dropped it so many years ago. I never would have imagined they'd keep the torches burning."

"So it's bad?"

"I'd say very bad. Except for Plummy. She absolutely doesn't get it, and she's not particularly interested, either. She just shrugs the whole thing off and goes to school."

"Did you ever ask your mother, you know,

what it's all about?" Not that I would blame him for a minute if he hadn't.

"She poked me and told me to mind my own business."

I fished my sunglasses out of my purse and stuck my elbow out the open window. I loved having somebody else drive. "I don't care," I said, leaning my head back. "Tomorrow, yes. Today, I am through with the whole thing."

Romeo reached over the gearshift and squeezed my hand.

"Would you like a Nib?" I asked him.

He nodded. I opened up the package and we ate them thoughtfully, one at a time. We commented on the price of blossoming cherry boughs as we took the expressway north to New Hampshire. We told each other stories of vacations we had taken as children and the vacations we had taken years later with our own children. We talked of the years we were broke and the years we were flush. We talked about how to raise a first-rate orchid. It was just past nine-thirty in the morning, and I thought that if nothing else were to happen from now until sundown, it would still be one of the happiest days I had had in years.

After crossing the New Hampshire state line, we took the first exit to Salem and drove on to Canobie Lake Park. Although I had promised to take Tony and Sarah there this summer, I hadn't been to the park myself since the girls were in grade school.

"I know this may seem crazy," Romeo said, "but it's totally different coming here if you don't have kids."

"What, you just come out here with no kids?"

"No, I bring my grandkids, but I always imagined it would be really different without kids."

Everything was different if you didn't bring the kids. I was always nervous in amusement parks—the revolting food you ended up eating, the creepy-looking carnies, the kids shooting off in every direction. It took exactly one second to lose them for good. I thought of it as a dangerous place full of dark hazards I had never imagined.

But in the daylight, my two girls grown and my grandchildren safely at home, Canobie Lake Park seemed remarkably wholesome, if slightly tattered. The sawdust was clean. The ticket taker was a chubby woman about my age who wasn't exactly warm (it was New Hampshire, after all) but was hardly menacing. The sky looked especially bright over the wooden spine of the roller coaster. In short, Canobie Lake Park appeared to me to be beautiful and romantic, which just goes to show it's not where you're at, it's who you're with.

"We don't open till ten," the woman said from inside her booth. It must have been true. We seemed to be the only ones there. "You can go ahead in, but I don't want you stirring up any trouble."

"What kind of trouble, exactly?" I asked.

The woman leaned forward and gave us each a bracelet to wear that would entitle us to go anywhere and do anything, absolute freedom. "There's no kind of trouble I haven't seen in this place. I want you to stay clear of all of it."

We went in. We were getting away from trouble, not looking for it.

"Does your family know you're here?" I asked Romeo.

Romeo shook his head. "I just snuck out. Sixty years old and I'm sneaking again. I haven't had any reason to sneak in a long time." He kissed me.

"I wonder what would have happened if

we had met when we were young," I said, staring out at the beautiful day in front of me—the blue sky, the white dipping clouds, the cotton-candy smell of the air. "I mean, what if you had come up to me at that party in eighth grade? It could have happened. We lived in the same town, our families were in the same business. What would have happened if we had fallen in love in high school?"

"The same thing that happened to Tony and Sandy, only worse. We didn't handle it well with our kids, but our parents, they were from another generation. They would have killed us. Your father would have killed me and my mother would have killed you."

"Poked to death."

"I'm not even sure if I'm kidding. That was very serious hate. My mother had a hard enough time with Camille, who was Italian. Her mother played hearts with my mother. Her father was our butcher, and she still didn't think Camille was the right girl for me."

"But she was," I said.

He smiled. "Camille was the right girl for me. There will never be another Camille. Just like there'll never be another Julie."

I felt a pang of jealousy, not that he had

loved her so much, but that my marriage hadn't been like his. I wished I could say something kind about Mort. I wished I could say, Boy, there were years we were great. It just wasn't true. There were plenty of years we were fine, maybe even good, but Mort and I were never great.

"So, it was better that we didn't meet then."

"My family doesn't like you now, but at least they don't want to kill you."

I thought about mentioning his son Joe, who certainly seemed capable of killing me if he took a mind to, but why spoil the day? "Do you ride the rides?" I asked him.

Romeo stood behind me and put his arms around my waist. He bent over to put his chin on my shoulder. "I think about it," he said softly into my ear. His voice made me shiver. "I used to when I was a kid. One of us would steal our parents' car keys and we'd drive up here late at night, jump over the fence. We'd buy one ticket for the roller coaster and then we'd just refuse to get off. We'd hold onto the bars and dig in our heels. They would have had to get a saw and cut us out of that thing. Then after the first couple of rides they'd quit trying to fight us and they'd just leave us on all night. We'd ride over and over and over again. I'd go until I couldn't feel my hands anymore."

"Bad kids," I said, feeling strangely breathless as his hand slid under the back of my sweater. "My father would have been right to keep me away from you."

"You want to try it?"

"She told us at the front not to make any trouble."

"I'm not talking about staying on forever, I'm talking about once."

I'd never been on a roller coaster. I had always been the one to stay on the ground and hold the popcorn bags. Not that anyone made me do it, it was just the role I chose for myself. They scared the living daylights out of me, but not as much as sushi. "Sure," I said. "Anything once."

chapter twelve

That was how things started. It was the roller coaster and then the Scrambler, the Zipper. There were only a handful of Nibs in my stomach to contend with and I held them down bravely. We took it all on. When we wanted to scream, we screamed. We held each other's hands and raised them over our heads. We went back to the roller coaster. The world spun in dazzling colors—yellow tents, black-haired children, dull grass, gold streamers. All of it merged, separated, re-configured. We stumbled to the Paratrooper. We did loop-de-loops and hung upside down suspended from our harnesses. We did not care. Gravity had no effect on us. My inner ear gave up and stopped trying to fight me. I no longer knew when I was right side up or upside down; even after the crowds came and we had to stand in lines, there was nothing in my head that was still. And it felt right. Now my physical self matched my life. My body became the metaphor. I was reckless, disoriented, thoroughly spun. I was drunk with confusion and licorice and desire. As soon as the young man with the dagger and heart tattoo and the ten A.M. whiskey breath locked us in our cage, we were at each other like two mammals that deserved to be locked in a cage. We pawed and groped our way across each other's bodies for as long as the price of admission allowed. Sometimes when the ride was over the guy would leer at us through the bars and yank back the controls that shot us up again toward the sun. One time the Zipper jerked backward twenty feet above the ground and I cut my lip on Romeo's forehead. There wasn't a lot of blood and it did not slow us down.

By noon I could no longer put together full sentences. "I think I need . . ." I tried to say what it was I needed, but I no longer knew.

"Rest. I need to rest," Romeo said. There was a little bruise coming up on his forehead.

He took my hand and we stumbled to the far side of the park. "Do you play Fascination?"

"What is it?"

"All you need to know is that you sit down and nothing moves."

The idea sounded so wonderful that tears actually came to my eyes.

The Fascination Parlor was some combination of skee ball, tic-tac-toe, and bingo. We cashed in bills for a handful of quarters and took two red vinyl stools at the end of long steel cages.

"This is where you win me cheesy stuffed animals that I keep in my bedroom," I said. "Nora always had a hundred of those things. Every guy she ever met won her a highly flammable stuffed dog."

"I'm not going to win you anything," he said, feeding two quarters into the slot. "I've always been rotten at Fascination, and right now my head is so screwed up I don't think I could tie my shoes."

"Good."

He tossed a rubber ball up the rubber ramp and into the cage. Sure enough, it hit one wall and then the other and then came bouncing back to him.

"That's something," I said. "Do you bowl?"

"About like this, except the ball never rolls

back to me." He threw up another, which reached the same conclusion by following a completely different path.

"Are you doing this to be amusing?"

"Nope." He threw again, this time whipping his wrist to the side to get a spin on the ball. It dropped into a hole on the bottom and disappeared. "I'm just unbelievably bad. I'm not just pretending to be bad so you'll feel sorry for me."

With every loss I found myself more profoundly attracted to him. He seemed so happy to lose. Mort would have stormed off four quarters ago, making it clear to everyone within earshot that the whole thing was rigged and nobody could win no matter how good they were. He would be demanding to speak to the manager about now. Mort could manage to wheedle a refund from even the scariest guy in the park.

Romeo gave me the quarters. "Go to work," he said.

I picked up the rubber ball and sank it in the middle square.

"Oh my God," he said. "You're a ringer. I've brought a ringer to Canobie Lake."

"I have good hand-eye coordination." I sank the next one in the upper left-hand hole. Actually, I don't know what I had—dumb luck maybe. In all honesty the game just didn't seem that complicated.

"So tell me about Nora. She sounds like a tough girl."

"Very tough." Ball three.

"So how'd she turn out?"

"She married an incredibly nice tax attorney and makes a fortune selling real estate. She drives a Lexus and wears good jewelry."

"I always wondered what happened to the tough girls," he said.

"Number Seven!" the caller said. "Number Seven wins the prize."

I had to check my seat to see if I was seven. When did I get to be so lucky? I told Romeo he had to pick the prize. After all, if he had won, he would have given it to me. He chose a stuffed cat with a small stuffed fish in its mouth. The fish had a huge smile on its face, as if it was thrilled to be devoured alive. "My granddaughter will like this," he said. "She has a thing for cats."

"Does she have a cat?"

Romeo shook his head. "That's one of my mother's primary rules—no cats." Should I worry about a man who lived with his mother? What difference did it make. I was never going to get anywhere near the old woman. Whatever relationship we had in the future would surely consist of long car drives and sneaking around. All around us people ate caramel apples and held hands. They took pictures of one another in front of rides. They screamed for their children and laughed outrageously at nothing. They wore long, thin balloons wrapped around their heads and walked invisible dogs on quivering, empty leashes. Romeo had one arm around my shoulder and one arm around the stuffed cat he called Tiger. This was a wonderful day, but it was as little like anything in my real life as I could possibly imagine. We went to a stand and bought clam fritters and Cokes. We ate standing up and when we were finished, we went back and ordered fried clam rolls and ate them, too.

"Hey," I said, wiping the fine coating of seafood from my mouth with a paper napkin. "Not to spoil the mood or anything, but do you have any thoughts on, you know, this? Us? I keep going over it and I keep coming up empty. The only really logical thing to do is quit before we get started, but then I think we've already started."

He tightened his grip on me. I could feel

the muscles in his arm go hard against the back of my neck. He kissed the top of my head. "Part of me says my family comes first," he said. "That's the primary law with the Cacciamanis and I believe in it. I can't stay with you because I don't want to hurt my mother and I especially don't want to hurt my children. The other part of me says to hell with that. I've been a good guy all these years, a team player, and I want to do what I want to do. Anyway, we're not hurting them. You're not a bad person. You're not going to tear my family apart."

"I don't think Nora is speaking to me, and Sandy is speaking to me, but she's profoundly disappointed in my actions. I don't know how long I'm going to be able to hold up under that kind of pressure. I mean, you and I aren't going to run off to Belize. We're not going to ditch our kids, never see our grandkids again."

"Maybe, over time, they'd get used to us together."

But neither one of us said anything to that. Every interaction I had with Cacciamanis, other than Romeo, only made things worse. Instead of coming to the conclusion that this was all a silly tradition, I was starting to think my mother and father were right. It wasn't just that his sons thought I was a monster, I was beginning to think they were monsters, too. I'm sure they were perfectly decent to other people, but to me they were little more than a looming mafia.

"Look," I said, pointing to a tent up ahead. "That's what we need, spiritual guidance." That's what the tent said, PSYCHIC READINGS AND SPIRITUAL GUIDANCE. PALMS, TAROT, CRYSTAL BALL.

"Oh, Al loves to give sermons on those things."

"I suppose he's against them."

"Al thinks you should take your spiritual guidance from God."

"Al gets a vote in this?"

"He is my best friend and my priest. It gives him a kind of double authority."

"Well, Al doesn't have sex and he doesn't have children. We need extra help."

I was a great reader of horoscopes, if not a great believer in them. I loved the idea of being assessed. All I wanted was a second opinion from an unbiased third party. The un-seen person in the tent seemed as good a shot as any.

"I don't know," Romeo said, eyeing the

tent like it was a center for some cult religion that snatched up teenaged runaways and forced them into saffron robes.

"Hey, I rode the Zipper," I said. "I've made my leap of faith for the day. You need to make yours."

We walked over, and after a moment's indecision about how to proceed, I rapped on the wooden sign. A woman in her sixties who looked like every woman in my neighborhood stuck her head out from the flap. She had short salt-and-pepper hair, a light-blue pullover, a little pink lipstick. She smiled at us. "One minute," she said, then disappeared again.

So we waited, not saying anything, kissing to pass the time, until a skinny blond girl about fourteen years old ducked out from under the tarp and flew off like a bird to find her friends.

"Think of all the future she had to hear about," Romeo said. "At least we won't take long."

A hand with short nails and no rings shot out from under the flap and waved us in. It was cramped and dark inside. We had to stoop or our heads would have lifted up the center of the tent. There were two dozen

candles and a little electric fan. The fortune-
teller was wearing jeans and gardening
clogs. I was disappointed. I was hoping for
something a little more exotic.

"You wanted Mata Hari," she said brightly.
"I'm Ellen. I used to be Madame Zikestra,
but the wig and the robes drove me insane.
It gets very hot in here in the summer."

"No, you're fine," I said. "I mean, I'm sure
you're fine." Did she read minds or did everybody ask her the same question?

"I only do one at a time," she said pleas-
antly.

I shook my head. "This is a joint deal," I
told her. "What we need to find out, we need
to find out together."

She thought it over for a minute. "Okay,"
Ellen said. "But for the two of you it's going
to be twenty bucks."

"Really?" Romeo said.

"Amazing, isn't it?" Ellen said.

I reached into my purse and put a twenty
down on the table.

"There's only one chair," she said.

So Romeo and I split the chair, each of us
hanging one leg off the side. We were no
closer than we had been on any of the rides.

"All right, let's get something for your

money here. Let me see those hands." She appeared to be a distant cousin of the older Doris Day, all button-nosed and bright-eyed.

"Don't you want to hear the problem first?" I said.

She shook her head. "Hands."

We put both of our hands faceup on the table, four palms turned up to the dim light. Romeo had on his wedding ring and Ellen tapped it once. "You're not married," she said.

"Not to her," Romeo said.

"Not to anybody," Ellen said in a matter-of-fact tone. "Not to anybody alive, and we can't be married to the dead. That's the first thing I have to tell you."

Romeo looked more interested then.

She traced her nail lightly across my palms and then went to Romeo's, then back to mine. "Most days are very boring," she said. I thought she was talking about our lives, in which case she would have been right about that, too. "I sit in this tent and all these little girls come in. 'How many babies will I have?' 'Does he really love me?' 'Am I going to get a car for my birthday?' On and on and on. The things I see I could never tell them, anyway. They're only children, after all.

They don't need to know anything. They should have their happiness. For example, if you had come in here at fourteen," she said to Romeo, "you wouldn't have wanted to hear that you were going to fall in love with a very kind woman and that you'll have seven children together and one of those children will die when she is a little baby. No boy at fourteen could make sense of that. Marriage, children, death—what would it even mean? I couldn't tell you that later on your wife was going to get breast cancer and die. To know all of that before would be un-bearable." She shook her head in sympathy for it all. "If you had heard it and believed me, you would have thought it would be im-possible to survive. But people survive ter-rible things. Now all those facts are history. Now I can tell you the truth. But if I had told you then, it would have been cruel."

Romeo closed his hands together like a book.

"Oh, come on. Don't do that," she said, and patted his hands. "Don't make me feel bad for talking. It's already happened, I didn't do it. It's good to see people who've had some life, people who want to know true things."

But I wasn't sure I did want to know. I wanted the carnival act, the fashion magazine horoscope: long life, true love, a bundle of money. I wanted Madame Zikestra. I wanted twenty dollars' worth of reassurance that everything was going to be fine. I knew I was going to die, that my girls would die, Tony and Sarah, all of us eventually. I had a general understanding of the order of life. That didn't mean I wanted the details.

"I think we should go," I said, but I didn't even try to stand up.

She ignored me. "Open your hands again," she said to Romeo.

He did what she told him.

"There are so many funny things here, the two of you. It's like a hall of mirrors. When I see your hands, I get the strongest sense of memory, like I've seen these two sets of hands before. You're not in any hurry, right? I want to tell you a story. A long time ago, years ago, two children came into my tent, very young. I was still doing the whole magic fortune-teller thing then. They said they had to come in together. I set their hands up just this way and I saw an amazing thing: The two of them had the same lines. Not the little ones, not the details, but in the big things they were twined together. But they were young, and so on their lines they were way up here"—she touched the pad beneath the base of my finger—"just at the beginning. I felt very sorry for them because I could see that, unlike other young people, they really were in love but that this love would separate them and whip them all across the world before they came together again. Their lines were so much together. In their hands there was so much love and hate. Never underestimate the hate. It can lock you just as tightly. But I didn't tell them anything. I said what they wanted to hear—their parents would forgive them, there would be joy in their families, blah, blah, blah. It was true, in a manner of speaking, but it was so far away. They never could have stood the pain if I had explained it to them."

Ellen had the careful, cheerful tone of someone who was giving you very complex directions to the expressway.

"And now I see the same two hands. You were right to say you had to come together. You were right to wait until now. If I had seen the two of you at fourteen, it would have been the same story and I would have told you the same lie. But this is where you are, right down here." She touched my hand again, closer to the base of my palm. I still had a good inch, inch and a quarter of life left, but it chilled me to see how much of the line was gone. "All the storms are clearing now and the world is bringing you together again, as it should be. You know what Shakespeare said, 'A brawling love, a loving hate'? That's the two of you. Just don't ever regret the past. It was all for a reason. You loved your wife," she said to Romeo, and then she turned to me. "And you, so you had to wait longer for love, but you had your girls and so the waiting became another kind of love." Ellen looked so pleased to be telling us all of this.

I nodded. I felt physically ill. Maybe the rides were catching up with me. Mostly it was the awful and completely impossible notion of Sandy and Tony sitting in this tent some fifteen years ago.

"So what do we do?" I said. "About the brawl?"

"It's been a hell of a storm, but every storm in the world runs its course sooner or later. Two hands like these don't happen very often, if I can count from personal experience." She scooped up our hands and made them into a pile. "Love each other madly, do you understand what I'm saying?"

I suppose it was clear enough. At any rate, I would have agreed to anything if it meant getting out of there. Romeo picked up the stuffed cat. We said good-bye and stumbled out of the tent. The sudden shot of sunlight made my head ache instantly, like leaving a movie theater at two in the afternoon in July.

"I'm sorry," I said to Romeo. "I'm so sorry about that."

"Come on." He took my hand and we began to walk away from the tent and the midway at a brisk pace.

"Where are we going?"

"We're leaving."

I followed him to the car. I wanted to ask him about the baby he and Camille had lost. I wanted to ask him if he thought it was possible she was talking about our children, but I felt so awful about dragging him in there in the first place that I couldn't bring a single word to my mouth. I felt like I wanted to go to a dark place and sleep for a week. I felt that in exchange for information Ellen had taken every ounce of energy I had.

Five miles outside of Canobie Lake, we came to a little green-and-white motel called

the Sylvan Park. Romeo pulled into the parking lot and told me to wait for a minute. I
stared at the bushes, the cracked asphalt,
and tried not to think about anything at all.
After the minute was up, he came back with
a key and got behind the wheel again.
"Twenty-three," he said. He drove to the end
of the row and parked the car. We went into
the room and fell down on the bed without
turning on the lights. I didn't think it was
strange we had wound up here. I think it was
the only place for us to go. He rolled over
and held me close to him. "I found you," he
whispered into my hair. "I found you."

Even though my heart was full of passion,
the heat of the day had finally caught up with
me. The rides and the food and all of the
wondering what would come next covered
my face like a rag soaked in chloroform, and
I only struggled against it for an instant before giving in. Romeo and I passed out together, tangled up, face-to-face, fully
dressed, our feet hanging over the end of
the bed. It was as if someone had turned off
a switch and at the same instant we were
gone. Or maybe it was relief. Maybe we believed Ellen. We would be together, even if

we didn't know how, so we could rest now, finally.

Sleeping with someone is the ultimate intimacy, I think. Through sleeping we establish trust. When we had had all the sleep we needed, our mouths preceded us in waking. When we woke up, we were already kissing again. I let my shoes fall to the floor. I slipped out of my sweater and crumpled linen pants. Romeo took off his shirt and jeans. He touched the champagne underwear lightly with his fingers, he ran the palms of his hands over the cups of the bra, as if he had never seen anything so remarkable in his life. He was the one I was waiting for, I believed that, even though I had made different lives with other people. This was my reward, this day, this moment, for any good deed I had ever done in my life.

Sex stays with you, even in the years you never call it into service, in the months it never once occurs to you. It hibernates deep, maybe in the backs of your knees or behind your liver. At first it seems impatient, unbearable, tugging at you every minute. Then it settles down to a place so remote you can almost forget it. It turns the lights low and it waits. But when you call it up again, it's there, full of memory and response. Romeo's hands, Romeo's mouth, the lines of his naked legs, the warmth of his chest against my face— every corner of him brought me back to life. The feel of his stomach against my stomach, the sweet forgetfulness of where you leave off and the other person begins. We were the roller coaster now, the Scrambler, the Zipper. Love rolled us together and tossed us into the air. We were something bigger than gravity. We stretched into it, closed our eyes, held on to each other, held tight. There was so much time that sex had a chance to be every different thing. We tumbled and devoured. I hit my hip against the headboard. He pulled my feet into the air. We slowed down and memorized each other's fingers. I held his earlobe between my lips. He traced my eyes with his tongue. We made love so deeply that I felt the very shape of my body changing. I whispered. He sang.

Somewhere in it all, Romeo told me he loved me.

I returned the compliment.

* * *

In Somerville the houses were all dark, but my porch light was still on. We kissed good night.

"We never did come up with a plan," I said.

"We're the plan," he said. "The rest of it will just have to fall into place."

I got out of the car and waved. My bones felt soft. I felt like I could just slip underneath the door and float up to my bedroom. Instead I got out my keys and let myself inside. I turned and waved again and then flicked on the light in the hall.

There was someone sleeping on my sofa. The light seemed to wake him up, and Mort rolled over, stretched and smiled.

"Hey there, Julie," he said.

chapter thirteen

Mort liked that couch. It wasn't like I'd never seen him there before. In the old days he would stay up late, watching television or working on the books, and when he got tired, he'd stretch out, thinking he was going to rest his eyes for a minute, and then not wake up until I woke him up in the morning. Of course, later on when things were falling apart, the couch meant something else entirely. Either he refused to come upstairs or I told him he could sleep on the goddamn couch. One way or another, Mort and that couch had logged in a lot of hours together over the years. It had been reupholstered, but it was still essentially the same piece of furniture, which is to say that Mort did not look out of place there even though I hadn't seen him in five years.

"Ah, Mort," I said. What was there to say? Should I scream, yell? Certainly that would come, but at that moment I was still dreamy, tired and spongy with sex. My heart was too full of goodwill to throw a lamp, even if a thrown lamp was what the situation required. Besides, I was more than a little relieved that it wasn't one of those hulking Cacciamani boys come to murder me for corrupting their father. "Mrs. Roseman," he would say, yawning. "I have come to kill you, but I fell asleep while waiting. Just a moment while I fish my gun out from between your sofa cushions."

If I was going to find a strange man on my couch, Mort was a better choice than many. "You look good, Jules," he said admiringly. "A little rumpled, but good."

"And you've come to tell me this?" Why didn't this whole thing seem stranger to me? Even with the five-year lapse, I was still so used to talking to Mort. I had lived with him longer than anyone else, longer than I had lived with my parents. Suddenly I had a terrible thought: What if something had happened with Lila? What if he was here because he wanted me back? "What's going on, Mort?"

Mort sat up and stretched as if trying to realign his entire body. He was the most un-

abashed stretcher I'd ever seen. Even after
a nap on an airplane, he would throw his
arms over his head and roar. Then he would
roll his shoulders, scratch his stomach, give
his scalp several vigorous rubs with his fin-
gertips. "What did you do with the old
couch? Just couldn't wait to get rid of it,
huh?"

"That is the old couch. I had it reupholstered."

Mort looked beneath him as if he had just
sat down on a pizza. "I'll be damned," he
said. "I liked it the old way better."

"Mort, why are you here? My God, it isn't
one of the girls? You haven't come to tell me
something horrible?"

He shook his head. "Nothing horrible, or
at least nothing horrible in which you are not
an active participant." He was starting to
look righteous. He was waking up.

"Romeo?"

"Jesus Christ, Julie. Like there weren't
other guys to choose from? Nora called me.
She was sobbing on the phone. I have to
leave my life, fly all the way across country
to try and get things straightened out. Do
you ever stop to think about what you're doing to the girls?"

As of today I was starting to think of myself as lucky, maybe for the first time in my life. All those years I had conversations with Mort in my head. All those years I thought of what I should have said after it was too late. Now here was Mort, back on my sofa, presenting me with a chance to vent my spleen. I put down my purse and came into the living room. "What I'm doing to the girls? What I'm doing?"

"What you're doing," Mort said, not giving an inch.

"I'm a single, sixty-year-old woman getting on with her life, that's what I'm doing. I'm not married and neither is Romeo. We're not busting up any families, betraying any confidences. You want to talk about the girls? Let's talk about the girls, Mort. Let's talk about what the divorce did to them."

"You can't throw this off on my shoulders. This isn't about me."

"You're damn right it isn't about you." There went the love, the sleepy tenderness. "So get your sorry ass off my couch and get out of my house."

Mort got up off the couch. He looked good himself, I was sad to say. He was thinner. He was wearing nicer clothes than he had been when he left. "We'll talk about this tomorrow when you're a little more rational. When you haven't been out half the night on a date." He managed to get a very nasty spin on the word *date.*

I looked at my watch. "It isn't even midnight. And we have talked about this. We're not talking about this anymore."

Mort pointed his finger at me. I could see the veins bulging out on the sides of his temples where he had once had hair. "I'm not going to watch you throw my business and my family down the tubes over a stinking Cacciamani. I will stop you if I have to sign the papers to have you committed myself."

I opened the door. "Out." We had been here once before, this hallway, these words, only it was his sex life we were screaming about then.

"Grandma?" Tony called down from the top of the stairs.

"It's okay, baby." I shot Mort a fierce look, what he used to call my boiling stare. "I'm home. I'm sorry we woke you up."

"Is Grandpa still here?"

"You've seen the kids?" I said to Mort.

"What do you think, I snuck in and got on the couch?"

"He's right here," I called up to Tony. "We were just talking."

Tony came padding down the stairs in his pajamas. I loved to see him in his pajamas. I knew that he was going to get big soon, that he wouldn't be the little boy who came and got into bed with me in the mornings. "Hey, Grandpa."

"Hey, Killer," Mort said. Why would you call a child that?

"Are you going to spend the night?" Tony came over and looped himself in my arms.

"Grandpa's in a hurry," I said.

"I'm going to spend the night at Aunt Nora's."

"Are you coming back tomorrow?"

"I'll be here when you get out of school."

"And Lila?" he said suspiciously.

"Lila's here?" I said.

"She's at Nora's."

"She played poker with me," Tony said. "She's not very good."

"Here?" I said. "She came here?"

"I wanted to see Sandy and the kids," Mort said. "What was I supposed to do, leave her in the car?"

"Yes. You were supposed to leave her in

the car. Why are you bringing Lila out here, anyway?"

"She wanted to visit her friends and Nora sent us two plane tickets."

I put the heels of my hands over my eyes. "No more," I said, as quietly as possible so as not to frighten Tony. "Good night."

Mort leaned over and kissed Tony on the top of his head. "You're getting so big."

"You told me that already," Tony said.

Mort finally said good night and left. I put on the dead bolt and the chain. "You need to get to bed," I said to Tony. "School to-morrow."

"You and Grandpa don't get along."

I tilted my head to the left and then the right. "Not particularly, but it's nothing that you should be worried about."

"I can't believe he likes Lila better than you," Tony said.

And on that bright note we went upstairs.

The night I had planned went something like this: I go up to my room, maybe light a candle. I take off my clothes and think fondly of every article before putting them in the hamper. Then I put on my nightgown, fluff up my pillows, and slide into bed. I don't go to sleep for a long time. I stop and take my time to rethink everything that happened. I ride every ride over again, I play Fascination, I eat the clams. I want to think about the sex right away, but I don't let myself, I save it, and when I've thought over every other aspect of the day, I remember the Sylvan Park motel. I think about nothing but that for at least an hour. I replay every second of happiness over in my mind. I make constructive plans for our future. I revel. That's what I was going to do.

Instead I tuck Tony back into bed and then go into my room and try very hard not to slam the door. Just who in the hell did Mort think he was showing up and telling me how I'm supposed to conduct my life in his absence? Who did he think he was sleeping on my couch, which I would now probably have to have covered again just so I didn't have to think of him on it every time I walked into the living room? I tore off my clothes, including my champagne underwear, and threw them into a ball at the foot of the bed. My hands were shaking as I dug through the medicine cabinet looking for my bottle of Excedrin P.M. I swallowed two blue pills without water, got into a T-shirt, and sat down on the bed. Lila in my house? Playing poker with my grandchildren? And what about Nora? It was one thing to deal with her harping disapproval, but for her to call in the National Guard to prevent me from having my one shot at happiness, that was more than I could easily forgive. How was I supposed to deal with her now? And, if it wasn't enough that it all had to happen, why did it have to happen *tonight?* Why did they all have to come in and chop down the best day I've had in I don't know when? I shut my eyes and tried to think of Romeo, but all I could see was Mort's bald head, his face contorted in righteous indignation. I used to feel so terrible when he looked at me that way, and while I still felt terrible, it was a different kind of terrible entirely.

My problems were too big for Excedrin, and by five o'clock the next morning I was downstairs relining the kitchen cabinets. I'd had the new shelf paper for about a year and I knew it was the only thing standing between me and a total nervous breakdown. In the store I had thought it was incredibly cheerful, yellow with a pattern of tiny daisies, but now that the plates were on the countertops and I was setting it in, I thought the daisies looked like bugs, little scurrying bugs that would run beneath the dishes. What the hell did I care? Chances were good that tomorrow morning I would feel like doing the whole job over again.

"This is bad," Sandy said when she came downstairs at six. "I haven't seen you paper the shelves since you and Dad were splitting up."

"Well then, it's time. Does this look like bugs to you?"

Sandy went up on her toes and peered down at a shelf. "Sort of."

I got my sponge and smoothed down the wrinkles.

"So is this because you had a bad time with Mr. Cacciamani yesterday or because you know that Dad is in town?"

"Dad and Lila," I corrected. "And Nora bought the plane tickets."

"Not to be a turncoat or anything, but I do want to tell you that I didn't have anything to do with this. I mean, I'm sure you know I didn't have anything to do with it financially, but I didn't know about it until they were on the plane coming out here."

"I appreciate that." I got down and started to cut another piece of paper.

"Are you sure you should be using a razor blade?"

"I'm not going to kill anyone, if that's what you mean."

Sandy sighed and nibbled thoughtfully on the top of her thumb. "So are you going to see Dad?"

"I saw him last night."

"He came back?"

"He was on the couch when I got home. There's coffee there if you want some."

Sandy shuffled over and got herself a cup of coffee. "He shouldn't have done that. He said good night, he left. I didn't want you to get ambushed. Did it go very badly?"

"Would you want to come home from a date in the middle of the night and find Sandy Anderson asleep on your couch?"

"I'd be so grateful to have a date, I doubt I would have cared." Sandy smiled at me. "I do get your point, though. How was your date, anyway?"

At the very thought of it I slumped down and threw aside the paper roll. "The date was great. Not that I can remember it very well now."

"Where did he take you?"

I eyed my younger daughter. "Honey, I

don't mean to sound paranoid, but this is just between you and me, right?"

A cloud passed over Sandy's face and a hurt look set in. "I was trying to show some interest. If you don't want to tell me, don't."

"I'm sorry," I said. "It's just that with everything that's going on—"

"I'm not Nora."

"Of course you're not Nora."

"I don't like this whole Cacciamani business. I think they're a bunch of thugs, but I'm trying to respect your choices. I should just stay out of it." Sandy put her coffee cup down on the table. "Forget I asked." She walked out of the kitchen and when I called her name she did not come back.

Canobie Lake Park, I wanted to say. We went to Canobie Lake Park.

I cleaned up the paper scraps and put the plates back where they belonged. Then I got dressed and went to work. It was barely light outside and I had already blown it at home. I liked to go in early on Mondays anyway so I could get all the new flowers unloaded and in their buckets before the customers came in. By ten o'clock, when I flipped the sign on the door to OPEN, the kids would be in school, the store would be ready, and Sandy would have forgiven me, I was sure of it. It seemed like I had completely lost my ability to say the right thing anymore.

I came in the back door and as soon as I was inside the shop, I felt better. I ran my hand over the wooden workbenches my father had built, looked at all my stripper and scissors and clippers hung neatly up on the Peg-Board on the wall. It was more my home than my house was. It was the place that always calmed me down. Inside of Roseman's I was a little girl with a watering can. My mother was young and beautiful, my father was whistling. I was the envy of all of my friends. I lived in a world made completely of flowers. I brought flowers to my teachers. I wore flowers in my hair. Even when I was a teenager and worked in the store, it was a happy time, or at least that's the way I remember it. The years I was married I hardly ever came here, so I didn't associate the place so much with Mort. When I took it over again, it was like coming back to my family. I became a Roseman again. I understood, I guess, why my father thought I couldn't take care of the business, and God knows I hadn't done a brilliant job, but I wished he could have seen me trying. I wished he could have known that I loved the store like it was family.

When I went to the front to wash the windows, I saw a box lying flat on the sidewalk, pressed against the door. It was a florist's box—of which I had a thousand—with a huge yellow bow tied to the front. At first I wondered if it was some sort of weird return, though I didn't recognize the ribbon. I unlocked the door and brought the box inside. The sticker on the front said *Romeo's.* Written beneath it in handwriting I now recognized, it said *Keep Flat. This Side Up.* There was an arrow pointing up.

Flowers? No one had ever sent me flowers in my life. "Like bringing coals to Newcastle," my father liked to say whenever I asked him if he ever gave my mother flowers. But here was the box. My heart was beating like crazy. Romeo, Romeo. It felt too heavy to be flowers. I was careful to keep it flat. I took the box to the bench and slipped off the ribbon, thinking in a fit of sentimentality that I would keep it. Then I pulled off the lid.

Vegetables.

Vegetables like flowers.

The tiniest leaves of spinach I had ever seen lined the whole bottom of the box like

a light cloud of florist's tissue. At the top
there were two purple cabbages trimmed in
white. They were blooming, that was the only
word for it. Around them in a halo of red were
twelve small tomatoes, each one perfect and
round, then stalks of tender green asparagus
sprouting leaves of six miniature Japanese
eggplants. At the bottom of the box there
was a row of zucchini, then red new pota-
toes, then baby carrots, their fernlike tops
still intact. The note was on a white florist's
card that had *Happy Birthday* printed at the
top with a line drawn through it.

Carissima Julie,
Did you know you were a very hard
person to buy a present for at six a.m.
on a Monday?
I love you,
Romeo

There was an arrow and I turned the card
to the back. *When is your birthday, anyway?*
I will admit it, I held the card to my heart.
I dipped my face down to smell the asparagus. Could he have been at the front door
as I was coming in the back? Had I missed

him? Beautiful, beautiful vegetables. All was redeemed.

"Vegetables?" Gloria said.

"I know it sounds funny, but you should see them. It's art, I swear to God."

"Okay," she said, and I heard her take a sip of coffee over the phone. Gloria was nothing without coffee. "So was the underwear a hit?"

"Don't you want to hear about the day first?"

"I want to hear about the day second. I want to hear about the underwear first."

So I told her. I wanted to tell.

"Good for you, sweetheart. You waited a long time."

I told her about the park, the rides. I told her about Ellen and the Sylvan Park motel. I told her about Mort on my couch.

"Mort? Excuse me?"

"I'm not kidding. He was there when I got home. Nora sent for him and Lila so that he could talk some sense into me."

"I take it all back, you should be scared of Nora."

"Right now I'm just angry. Mort's bound to show up today. God, Gloria, it's like life is so good and so bad. How can it be that way all at the same time?"

"I think that is life by definition."

"Would you do me another favor?"

"To aid the course of true love or thwart your ex-husband, anything."

"I'm going to owe you big after this. If you decide to start running arms to South America or open a day-care center, you know I will do anything you ask me to."

"Name it."

"Go to Romeo's and tell him I got the vegetables. Tell him I'm crazy about the vegetables."

"Wouldn't it be easier to call and just hang up if you get the wrong Cacciamani?"

"I don't want to get him in any trouble."

"I think you sent me out on a very similar mission in tenth grade, but I'm willing to do it."

"You're an angel."

"What do you want me to say, exactly?"

"It doesn't matter," I said, knowing that Gloria and I were of the same mind on these matters. "Just go and talk about love."

chapter fourteen

Sandy was still sullen when she came to work at ten, but being that it was Monday, there was a lot to do and she had to get over it quickly. Actually, there wasn't as much to do as there should have been. Both of our flower shipments came up short, and since I had given everything left from the weekend to Father Al, there were no stragglers to back us up. There were no deliveries to go out on Monday mornings so we stayed in the shop together, unpacking the flowers we had and going over the plans for a big wedding the weekend after next. The bride wanted every flower in the synagogue to be a gardenia. It was not a small wedding.

"Does she have any idea how that place is going to smell?" Sandy said, crinkling up her nose. "I mean, I like gardenias, but people are going to be falling over in the aisles. Is she planning on providing oxygen tanks?"

"All I know is that I've ordered the flowers. Let's hope she doesn't change her mind. A thousand gardenias aren't so easily moved."

The phone rang and Sandy answered it and took the order. "What do you want on the card?" she asked, poising her pen over the tiny white card. "Okay, yes, 'Darling Maria, without you my life would have no meaning. You are the sun and the moon, the stars in the night sky.' Hang on, hang on, you're getting ahead of me." She flipped the card over. " 'In my life I have never known love like this before. I have waited for you since the beginning of time.' Wait. The card is full. Let me get another one. These are really small cards."

While Sandy continued to take dictation, Gloria swept into the store looking a little better than I thought was necessary. She was wearing a slim black skirt and low heels. Gloria was thinner than I was and she had great legs. I was wondering if I had made a mistake in sending her. Romeo didn't have to make Father Al promise to dress down when he came to see me. "Oh my God," she said. "I saw him. I was just there."

Sandy capped her pen and hung up the phone. "Saw who?"

Gloria shot me a look, but I figured there was no sense in putting all of us in a tight spot. "Romeo Cacciamani," I said. "I asked Gloria to go over and thank him for a present."

"He sent you a present?" Sandy said suspiciously.

"Come on," I said. I took them both into the cooler and pulled the lid off the vegetable box. I dazzled them with my dinner.

"Wow," Sandy said, extending one tentative finger to an eggplant. "Are they real?"

"They are."

"They're stunning," Gloria said. "You were absolutely right. For the rest of my life I'm going to feel disappointed when Buzz sends me flowers. Now can we get out of the freezer? I know you two are used to it, but I'm not."

We came out with the vegetable box. I didn't want to put the lid back on.

"And you had to send Gloria over to thank him?" Sandy said. "You can't even go and see him?"

"Not exactly," I said. "You know how his family feels about me, and he knows how you and Nora feel about him. We're trying not to step on too many toes here." Maybe

I was spelling things out a little too much, but I wanted a few points for sensitivity.

Sandy picked up an asparagus stalk, twirled it gently in her fingers. "A guy who'd do something like this . . ."

"Is a wonderful guy," Gloria said. "Julie, you were right not to go over there. Lord, the place is absolutely crawling with Cacciamanis. Frankly, I'm relieved that you're getting together with him, shall we say, later in life, because I would not have wanted to see you spend your youth with someone who clearly has such a weak grasp on the whole birth-control issue."

"What did he say?" Sandy asked.

"Well, the first trick was getting him alone. I told the thug at the cash register that I wanted to discuss the flower arrangements for my husband's funeral and that I would rather speak to the owner in a private place. Did you know he has an office? Why don't you have an office?"

I had a desk at the end of the workbench. It was fine. "You told him Buzz was dead?"

"I only told the first guy Buzz was dead. I told Romeo the truth when we were alone. That was the point, to see him alone."

"So what did he *say?*" Sandy repeated.

Gloria looked at her. "He said he was crazy in love with your mother, okay?"

"That's enough for me," I said.

"He said he's thinking maybe you could go to dinner in Newton tomorrow night. He says he doesn't know anyone in Newton. I told him we know everyone in Newton."

"Tomorrow night's my night with the kids," I said. "Maybe Wednesday."

"I can get a baby-sitter," Sandy said. "Nora could come over. Or Gloria. It's not the end of the world."

"Are you saying you're going to help me go on a date?" Gloria and I were both staring at her. If the answer was yes, I wanted a witness.

"I'm saying those are very nice vegetables," Sandy said wistfully. "You don't see something like that every day. That's all I'm saying. I'm going to go watch the store. You two talk." Sandy replaced the asparagus stalk carefully and left us alone.

"That's a girl you can trust," Gloria said. "She's warming to this."

"It comes and goes. Tell me, what did Romeo say?"

"Everything right. He was so glad I had come. He said he couldn't stop thinking about you. He had a wonderful time at Canobie Lake, though to hear him tell it, you drove up there, played a couple rounds of Fascination, and came home."

"It was something like that. Did you tell him about Mort?"

Gloria shook her head. "I figured what's the point in making the poor guy crazy? He's going to be worried, he's going to be jealous. I liked him too much for that."

I heard the bell on the front door and then Sandy's voice. "Hi, Dad."

There was a pause, some footsteps, and then Mort. "Would you look at this place? It's a dump. She's turned it into a dump."

"Speak of the devil," Gloria said. "Do you want me to stay?"

"Something tells me this one isn't going to be quick. I think you've done enough for one day."

"It's not that I want any harm to come to Mort, or even to my own ex-husband exactly, but I don't think they should be allowed to walk around, popping up anytime they feel like it. What I envision is something called Planet of the Ex-Husbands. Let all that money the government spent on NASA be put to good use. We just shoot them off into space."

"I don't think that's a bad idea."

"Mom?" Sandy called. "Could you come out here, please?"

Gloria went first, smiling and holding her arms out to Mort. "Mort!" she said. "Imagine us both showing up at Roseman's."

Mort kissed her on the cheek and gave her a squeeze on the shoulder. "You look good, Gloria." He said it in the exact same tone of voice he had used to tell me that I looked good, like he was both surprised and humbled by our beauty. I wanted to kick him. "How's Buzz?"

"Just great. The reports of his death have been greatly exaggerated. In fact, I'm off to see him right this minute. The next time you're coming to town, let me know first." Gloria gave Sandy a kiss and waved good-bye.

"So I guess she's in on this whole thing," Mort said, watching her walk away. "Your great conspirator. She must be loving this."

"Nobody is loving this," I said. With Gloria gone I felt less confident. It seemed like she had taken all of the air in the room with her when she left.

Mort started pacing the shop from corner to corner. "I see you're killing the shop. Is that part of the romance? He talks you into tanking the business so he can be the only game in town?"

"Mort."

"Where are all the flowers? Can you tell me that? This is a flower shop, you're supposed to have flowers."

"There was some kind of trouble with the shipment, all right? It's just today. You want to tell me in all the years you worked here you never had a problem with delivery?"

"I had my problems, but I was always on the phone yelling at somebody. Who have you called this morning?"

I hadn't called anyone. The vegetables came and then Sandy and then Gloria. I didn't even think about it. "I'll run my store my way."

"Your store. That just galls me. Your father promised me this store. He said it was my store."

"On the one unspoken condition that you not run off with a bridesmaid, Mort. For God's sake, how much can you expect?"

"I expected fair treatment. I gave this place my life."

"Well, at least you know how it feels," I said.

Sandy cleared her throat. "Mom, Dad, you know this is fascinating for me, but if you don't mind, I think I'm going to go now." Somehow she had made it all the way over to the door without our noticing.

"Ah, honey," Mort said, "you shouldn't get so touchy. Your mom and I are just talking."

"Talk all you want," Sandy said, "I just don't want to hear it."

She went through the door like a bullet, setting the bell off into a veritable symphony of jangles. I stood and watched her pack of curls bounce away in the sunlight. Sandy's hair went a long way toward giving her levity. No matter how hard she tried to storm away, she always bounced.

"Sandy's right," I said, "we shouldn't be talking like this, especially not in front of her."

But Mort just waved his hand. "Both of those girls need to toughen up. They're too sensitive."

"Nora needs to toughen up?"

"You don't understand Nora. She's all jelly on the inside."

I had certainly never considered that possibility before, and I wasn't sure I liked the picture. "Maybe I don't understand." I went over and moved two pots of hydrangeas out of the late-morning sun. "But you're not the one to explain it to me." I stopped and looked at Mort, my husband for more than half my lifetime. Mort, whom I had known at twenty. Mort, who to this day believed I had lost my virginity to him. "Mort, just go, okay? We're only going to get into a horrible fight. We've about gotten to the point where there's some serious water under the bridge between us. We've both gotten on with our lives. What's the good of opening things up again, fighting over the flower shop or the girls? We've already had all those fights. If you go now, you and Lila can have a nice vacation in Boston. See the kids, don't see me, tell Nora whatever you want to tell her. That isn't such a bad deal, is it?"

"So you'll stay away from the Cacciamani, is that what you're telling me?"

I sank down into the little wicker chair. "How in the world could that be what I'm telling you?"

"Because that's what this whole thing is about. Not the store and not the girls. Your father didn't keep his promise to me, but I'm keeping my promise to him. He told me that

Rosemans and Cacciamanis had to keep away from each other. It was my job to make sure they did. You know that whole business with Sandy nearly broke your parents' hearts. I know it took five years off your father's life."

"I told you not to tell them."

"You don't understand the way the world works, Jules. This Cacciamani bastard isn't just some guy I don't get along with. I've seen him operate for years, first with his old man and then with his rotten pack of boys behind him. These aren't your average bad people. They're despicable. I think they're probably mafia."

"The Flower Mafia, Mort? Give me a break. What did the Cacciamanis ever do to you? Do you even have any idea what this whole feud is about?"

"What it's about?" Mort said. "What it's about? Julie, what rock have you been living under all these years? It's about business. It's about them smearing our name all over town, saying we used old flowers for weddings. Saying we went to the cemetery and picked up our bouquets after funerals, for Christ's sake. They kept me out of Rotary. They used some pull to keep us out of the phone book one year. The phone book! Do you even know what that means? And like I said, it didn't start with Romeo. Not hardly. It goes back to his old man and that evil, evil bag he was married to, may they rot in hell."

"Not so fast. She isn't dead yet."

"Is that possible?" Mort shrugged. "Then they're waiting for her. They're sharpening up the pitchforks. Those people undermined us in every way that was possible. They'd call our big accounts and say we had canceled, that they were going to be doing the flowers. And God forbid a Monday morning ever rolled by when I wasn't here to meet the shipment. Every rose in the bunch would have its head twisted off."

Okay, that one I believed. I had seen a Cacciamani behead a plant before. "So if this is true, some of it, any of it, how many of those exact same things did my dad do right back to them? And what did you do? Do you expect me to believe the Cacciamanis threw all the punches and the Rosemans stood there and took it?"

Mort looked like he couldn't possibly be hearing me right. Normally I'd be upset if I didn't have any customers on a Monday morning, but today I was relieved. "Is that what you want to believe? Is that what you'd want your family to do, never hurt your precious Romeo? Of course I went after them. So did your folks. When we got hit, we hit back. That's called life, Julie."

"Life, fine, but then after a couple of generations who throws the first punch? Are you reacting or are you going out there to nail them?"

"What in the hell difference does it make? These are Cacciamanis we're talking about. All that matters is that we get them before they get us."

"But don't you see, Mort? It's a game. They played dirty, we played dirty. Everybody hates everybody. But if we decide to stop it, if both sides choose not to fight anymore, then the game is over. It's that simple."

"That simple if you were playing with fairminded people, which you're not. Consider a hypothetical here. Say Sandy started writing letters to a murderer in prison. Say after some time she came to us and said, 'Mom, Dad, Spike has changed and he's a wonderful guy now and I'm going to marry him in prison.' Wouldn't you jump in front of a train to try and stop that one?"

I wanted to say that I would trust my

daughter's good judgment, but the scenario didn't seem completely implausible to me. "Yes, but if what you're saying—"

"What I'm saying is that love blinds us." For a second his voice was soft. He came over and leaned against the counter. Mort looked like he was as tired out by this whole thing as I was. "We don't always see the whole picture. That's why the people who love us, the people who are responsible for us, have to step in and save us sometimes."

"Oh, Mort, I don't expect you to understand this, but I don't need saving. When you ran off with Lila, I thought the same thing. I didn't believe she wanted what was best for you. But it was your life and you were entitled to your own mistakes."

"I'm not going to let this drop, Julie."

"You're going to have to. You live in Seattle, and sooner or later you have to go home. I really don't want to fight with you. I just want you to go."

Mort sighed and looked around the shop. Without a moment's hesitation he picked up the best pot of purple cyclamen from a bunch of pots on a low platform and put it next to the cash register. "Got to get them up to eye level. You know that Lila and I have a shop now. At first I didn't think it was right, I thought I needed to move on to something else, but I'll tell you, you can't walk away from flowers, not after you've been doing it your whole life. It gets in your blood."

I asked him how business was doing.

"It's a trade-off. A lot more money out there, but it's all a lot more expensive, too. One fancy party for Microsoft and we make more money than this store brought in in a month. Lila picked up on the business fast. She has a real good head for flowers."

"I'm glad to hear it."

Mort went back to the cooler and pulled out the bucket of Siberian irises. "You should be moving these."

"I just got them today."

"Irises just don't last. You have to turn them over."

I wanted to stop him, but he was right. Besides, it was a relief not to be fighting for a minute.

Mort put his hands on his hips and surveyed the store, the lord of all he saw. "This is a great place, do you know that? The space, the light. You couldn't find a place like this in Seattle. It could use some updating, but the whole feel of it . . . I always had a real connection here. From the first time you brought me in, I really believed that one day this was all going to be mine. I loved this shop."

"I know you did."

"Let me see the books, Julie. I know you're running the whole thing into the ground."

"It's my store now. Forget about it."

"I know it's your store, but I still have feelings for the place. I'm not asking for so much. Just give me a couple of hours."

"Look, Mort, I'm trying to get you out of my business, not deeper into it."

Mort rubbed his eyes. "If the place was on fire, would you turn away my bucket of water?"

"Don't be stupid."

"No, *you* don't be stupid. I might be able to help you put out the fire. Why don't you try loving Roseman's more than you hate me."

It was only my vanity that stopped me. I wanted Mort to think I was shooting out the lights. But the truth was that he was great with the books and I was turning them into soup. He knew things about working out orders that I had never come close to mastering. He was right, we were going down. I did need help. "Okay," I said finally, waving him back toward the desk. "You know where everything is, anyway. Nothing has changed."

"Oh, Julie," he said, with what I thought was some sadness in his voice. "Everything's changed."

chapter fifteen

The one good thing about having Mort look over the books was that it took his mind off of Romeo. "Jesus!" he would yell while I was waiting on customers.

The customers would look toward the back of the store. Some appeared frightened, others were simply confused. "He's trying to move the desk," I said calmly. "It's very heavy."

At one point Mort tore open the curtain that separated the front of the shop from the back. "What are you trying to do?" he said. "Kill us? Lose everything?"

"Kill me," I said, pointing to my chest. "Not us. It's mine to lose."

"Well, congratulations on your newfound liberty because you've lost it."

"How was I supposed to know what to do? For thirty-four years you never let me in the store, and then you up and run off to

Seattle with Lila. There wasn't time to take a course in accounting. I had to get to work."

"That's why you pay people, Julie. They're called accountants. They're for people who don't know what the hell they're doing."

"With what, Mort? You got the money, remember? That was the deal. The house is mortgaged up to the gutters. I've got a loan on the shop."

"You took a loan against Roseman's!"

I hadn't meant to tell him, but in the next thirty minutes or so he would have found out, anyway. I felt my eyes welling up with tears. I was overcome with shame and guilt because I knew what he was saying. I had mortgaged my parents' store, borrowed against the very thing they had worked their whole lives to pay off. "I didn't know what else to do."

"You should have called me." Mort was seething. Tears had no effect on him.

"I wasn't going to call you. You know that."

Mort closed the curtain again and went back to work. I did a little watering and made a note to myself to order more floral life. What would happen if I lost Roseman's? Who would I be without the flower shop?

Nora was always going to be fine, and she didn't care a thing about flowers anyway, but I wanted it to be there for Sandy if she wanted it. She might not want to be a nurse or she might get tired of being a nurse someday. She could make the business work. I wanted it to be there so that one day she could give it to Tony and Sarah. They'd make a perfect combination. Tony would run a tight ship in the back and Sarah would charm the socks off of everybody up front. To think I could have frittered away the only legacy my family had out of sheer incompetence, it absolutely killed me. I went into the back. "Just forget about it," I said to Mort. "You can't fix it. Go home to Lila. She must wonder where in the hell you are."

Mort didn't look up. He was punching on a calculator just as fast as his fingers would go. He had a pencil behind each ear. "Leave me alone."

"I'm serious, Mort. Forget it. It isn't your problem."

"It is my problem. Now get out there and sell some goddamn flowers."

I closed the curtain. I felt very weepy now. The way I saw it, I had lost or would eventually lose my marriage, my business, my daughters, and Romeo. Somewhere my parents were looking down on me and shaking their heads in despair.

Despite the lack of flowers, the lack of Sandy, and my generally glum demeanor, business was pretty good. At one o'clock Mort asked me to go out and get him a sandwich and said he'd watch the store. I didn't even have to ask him about lunch. I knew full well he wanted roast beef with horseradish on an onion roll, extra pickles, no chips, and a diet Sprite.

I walked the extra block to the sandwich shop that was careful to trim the fat.

"Why can't Lila ever get this straight?" Mort wondered aloud, looking into the sack. Then he went back to work.

I bought myself a yogurt but then didn't even have the appetite for that. I stuck it back in the cooler behind some daisies and resumed my worrying.

There was always a convenient lull around two when Sandy usually left, and then a short flurry of activity from five to six when husbands and boyfriends stopped in for a ready-made bouquet on their way home from work. To make a sweeping generalization, women bought flowers during the day and men bought them once the sun started to go down. From two to five was usually when I worked on the books, but Mort was still back there, swearing and moaning under his breath. Today the bell rang at two-thirty and in walked a very nervous looking Romeo Cacciamani. He was wearing gray pants and a nice white shirt with rolled-up sleeves. He looked almost unbearably handsome.

"My God," I said, my voice automatically dropping to a whisper. "What are you doing here?"

"Your friend Gloria said this was when Sandy went to pick up her kids from school. Is this all right? Is Sandy here?"

I glanced behind me and moved quickly to the front of the store. I kissed him. I couldn't help it. I was so glad and so sorry to see him. "She isn't here, but you have to go. Really. She could be back any second."

"I'm sorry. I know I shouldn't have come. I've been driving around the block for half an hour telling myself not to come. But I had to see you."

"I loved the vegetables."

"Did you? I just didn't know what to send. I wanted to buy you something big, like, say, California, but there wasn't time." He put his arms around me. It felt like heaven. "What about dinner tomorrow?"

"Sure," I said. "I can work something out, but you have to go now." I couldn't believe I was getting the words out of my mouth. I wanted him to stay and stay. I wanted to tell him everything that was happening. I wanted to tell him everything that had ever happened to me in my life.

"Is everything all right? You seem so upset."

"It's a stressful time," I said, and then, as if to prove my point, Mort came out from behind the curtain with three spiral ledgers. He dropped them.

"Cacciamani!" he yelled. "Get your lousy mitts off my wife."

Wife? I thought. Where was Lila?

"What's he doing here?" Romeo asked, his tone more curious than alarmed. He kept his mitts firmly on me.

"None of your goddamn business what I'm doing here. Now get out before I set you on the curb in pieces."

Romeo seemed to smile a little in spite of himself. "I haven't heard that one in a long time."

"I swear to God, Cacciamani, get out of

here now. You do not want to get into it with me."

"Of course I don't want to get into it with you. What in the hell is your problem, Mort?"

"My problem? My *problem?* You're my *problem,* buddy. You always have been. Except when I was here, you knew enough to stay away. Now I'm gone and you're sniffing around my wife, ruining my business." Mort shook the few papers he was still holding in his hands. Somehow it seemed the two problems had become conflated in his mind. Now it was Romeo's fault that Roseman's was sinking, Romeo's fault that I wasn't sitting at home. The Red Sox's inability to play in the World Series—that was probably Romeo's fault as well.

Romeo scratched his head. "Your business? Your wife?"

"Well, they sure as hell aren't yours."

"Listen, Mort, enough with the tough-guy talk. We never got along. So what? This isn't a turf war."

"This is a turf war, if that's your terminology. I want you off my turf."

Romeo took a small step away from me, toward Mort. "You don't live here anymore, unless I've gotten the story wrong."

"Let me tell you, Cacciamani, you've got everything wrong." Mort came out from behind the counter.

"Look," I said. "This is a ridiculous mistake. Mort is visiting and Romeo is leaving. Let's just drop it."

"I'm not leaving," Romeo said. He looked somehow mesmerized, as if he was staring into the swinging watch of a hypnotist and couldn't turn away. Mort was taller than Romeo, but Romeo was built like somebody who could throw an ox through a wall, or at least he could have twenty years ago.

Mort nodded, the veins coming up. "Well, good. That's really fine, because you're the one I've been wanting to talk to, anyway. You just saved me a trip."

"Mort," I said in a tone used to soothe nervous Doberman pinschers. "Settle down."

"Stay out of this, Julie. You," he said, pointing at Romeo, "need to stay away from my family. I thought I had made that clear in the past, but maybe we need to go over it again. You stay away from Julie. You stay away from my girls. You stay away from my store."

"You can't tell him to stay away from me,

Mort, or the store." It wasn't that I was completely against him at that moment. He had spent the day trying to rescue my books. He was tired and hugely frustrated, and I liked to think that had this meeting taken place at another time it might have gone better.

Mort turned to me. "Are you on his side?"

"Please. Let's just all walk away from this."

"After everything he did to me?"

Romeo said, suddenly enraged, "Did to you? If he wants a fight, I'll give him a fight. I swear to God I had put the past in the past. I forgot what had happened." He turned toward Mort. "But if you want to bring it up, I'm sure I can make myself remember."

"A fight?" Mort said, his eyes bright as dimes. "You want to fight me?"

Who said these things? People screamed, they bullied, but fighting was something done only in the movies.

"If that's what you're looking for, come on."

No sooner were the words out of Romeo's mouth than Mort had the cyclamen in his hand and was hurtling it straight at Romeo's head. Mort had been state-ranked in baseball when he was in college, and in all his years in Somerville he played on a softball team. He could pitch a crumpled-up paper towel through a window. They called him The Arm.

It was a clay pot. I was especially sorry about that. It hit Romeo on the left temple and exploded into a fan of dirt, petals, stems, and terra-cotta shards. Romeo went down.

I hardly knew which way to go. Did I comfort Romeo or try and take Mort out? For all his fits of rage, I had never seen Mort strike another person. He didn't even spank the girls when they were little. I knelt beside Romeo. His head was bleeding spectacularly and I was trying to brush the dirt out of his eyes. I loved him. It was one of those moments in life when you're sure.

"Mort, you stupid son of a bitch, you could have killed him!"

I thought he was on the floor for the count, but at the very mention of being killed, Romeo, bleeding and coated in potting soil, rose up from the ground and flew at my ex-husband like a creature with wings. I don't believe his feet once touched the floor until he got his hands around Mort's throat and started beating his head into the counter.

Mort somehow pulled up an arm and landed a hook on the exact spot where Romeo's head was already split open.

Romeo, reflexively, brought up his knee.

I hadn't seen many fights in my life. A couple of brawls in Harvard Square. Two teen-aged boys in the street outside my store once. I called the police then. I was wondering if I should call them now. It never occurred to me that intelligent grown men still fought, and yet there I was watching it as if the whole thing were taking place underwater. I thought that fighting had rules. There were certain things people restrained themselves from doing. I was wrong. They were slugging, pulling. I think I saw Mort bite. The Siberian irises had been overturned and mashed into a soggy purple smear on the floor. They knocked over the card rack and smashed the African violets. "Stop it!" I screamed. "Stop it!"

With that simple command they fell apart, rolled away from each other limp and panting, bloody and dislodged. They were ready to stop. They had only needed someone to ask them. They lay on my floor amid the dirt and the blossoms, both of them unable to stand. In less than a minute they had both been ruined, the store had been ruined, I had been ruined. I went to Romeo, whose whole head was covered in blood. Both his forehead and his lip were bleeding now and his left hand was turned at an unnatural angle. He said my name and tried to touch his face to see if anything was left. There was a bright red pool forming under his head.

But it was Mort who really concerned me. At first glance, you'd say he was the better-looking of the two. I think most of the blood on him was Romeo's, but there was a horrible swelling on the side of his head where the skin was taut and shiny yellow. I couldn't get him to respond to me. He lingered in a mumbling, half-conscious state and then slipped out of it. I put my head down on his chest and listened to his heart.

Romeo dragged himself into a sitting position, wincing at every inch. "Dear Mother of God," he said, looking at me listening. "Tell me I didn't kill him."

"You didn't kill him," I said. "But I'm calling an ambulance."

Time happened in a dream. The hospital was very close, and yet it seemed like the second the phone was in the cradle, the ambulance guys were rushing through the door.

Because I had told them, when asked over the phone, that the cause of injury was a fight, they sent the police as well. Blue and red lights flashed brightly through the window of the store, and Ginger, the woman who runs the dress shop next door, came over to see if I'd been murdered.

"Do you know these men?" the young officer asked me as two paramedics started working on Mort and the third applied pressure to Romeo's head.

"Ex-husband," I said, pointing. "New boyfriend."

He nodded and closed his book.

"We've got a concussion here," the paramedic said of Mort.

"This one is losing a lot of blood," Romeo's paramedic said. "We've got to get going."

I thought he might put up an argument, but Romeo simply slumped down into the man's arms and allowed himself to be hoisted onto a stretcher. They already had Mort's limp body tied onto a gurney, and side by side, like bunk mates at camp, they were slid into the ambulance. I got in between them for the short ride, just to make sure nobody woke up and tried to get things going again.

I watched Somerville spin behind me out the back window while the ambulance wailed and cried. I had one hand on each of their chests, Romeo to my left and Mort to my right. They both had their eyes closed and their breathing was labored and sharp. I knew it would never be like this again, this minute when I was able to give a little comfort to both of them.

I had plenty of blood on me by the time we got there, and a good-looking doctor helped me out of the back and then asked me if I had been hit in the fight. I said no, though all of my actions seemed to disprove my statement. I was dizzy and confused. I'd read somewhere that there were people who do very well in the moment of crisis but then fall apart once the worst of it has passed. When I thought of Romeo's blood, I had to put my head between my knees to keep from fainting. Inside the emergency room they took Mort and Romeo off quickly. The nice policeman brought me a paper cup full of cold water and pointed to the pay phone.

"Call someone," he said.

I called Sandy. "Listen carefully," I said. I

told her to call Gloria to come and watch the kids. Then she should call Nora and come to the hospital. "Your father has been in a fight."

"The two of you were fighting?" Sandy said. "Fistfighting?"

"It was Romeo," I said. It didn't matter if she knew or Nora knew or any of them knew. It was over. No one could come back from something like this.

"How bad is it?" Sandy said, her voice tentative.

"Not bad like death. Not even bad like permanent injury. But bad."

"How's Romeo?"

"Um, I'd guess about the same. It's so hard to know. I have to call his family. He's pretty messed up."

"Don't call them until I get there," Sandy said pragmatically. "They're going to kill you."

I wasn't sure how Sandy planned on saving me from the impending wrath of the Cacciamanis, but it was sweet of her to think of me. I sat with the phone in my hand for several minutes before I pulled myself together and called the store.

"Romeo's," a voice said.

I asked to speak to Raymond Cacciamani. Despite our unpleasant first meeting, I remembered Romeo saying he was the most rational of his sons.

"You bet," the voice said, so cheerful, so helpful. It sounded like the place was packed. It sounded like they were having a party there. "Ray-mond."

There was a pause and I tried to keep from sobbing. A different yet very similar voice came on the line. "Raymond Cacciamani."

I cleared my throat. "Raymond, don't hang up the phone. There's been an accident and your father's in the hospital. This is Julie Roseman." I thought it was best to put that fact at the end.

"Somerville Hospital?" he said as if he was taking an order for a delivery.

"Yes."

Raymond hung up the phone. Personally, I would have asked a couple of questions. With that much information, for all he knew, Romeo was dead. I was planning on begging him to come alone. I was going to tell him it was only a cut and everything was fine. Too late for that. I didn't think there was any point in trying again.

I went to the nurses' station and made inquiries.

"Are you a relative?" the nurse asked without looking up.

"Ex-wife to one and friend to the other—girlfriend."

"So not exactly family in either case. Nobody's ready to have company right now, anyway. Why don't you just wait another minute?"

So I slumped down into a yellow plastic chair and I waited, waited for Nora and Sandy and all the Cacciamanis. Waited to pay the price for a little happiness.

chapter sixteen

A broken ex-husband, a battered new lover, two hysterical daughters, and a whole host of raging Cacciamanis—that was what I braced myself for. What I forgot, amazingly enough, was the one thing that would truly, deeply disturb me: Lila the wife. It was understandable, I guess, in my deranged mental state that I would suppress her, and yet when she clicked through the electric doors in her high heels, I felt the last bits of whatever inner glue I had holding me together give way. Lila Roth, both bridesmaid and bride. We had met before, or if not met, passed each other in the driveway while she was helping Mort move out and I was leaving so as not to watch. She wore cutoff denim shorts that day and a red halter top. I will remember that outfit on my deathbed. It's all transference, I know. Not one thing that had happened today could in any way be con-

strued as Lila's fault, and yet every fiber in
me blamed her as she pounded the white
tile floor toward me. Nora was close behind.

Lila was a blonde. Maybe real, maybe not.
Who was I to say? I wasn't her hairdresser.
She had a certain kind of thinness that
smacked of self-obsession. She was wearing eye shadow, her nails were shell pink,
she wore stockings with open-toed shoes,
her teeth were bleached a toilet-bowl white.
Need I go on? Not a single detail escaped
me.

"Did you kill him?" Those were her first
words to me. Her breath was sweet with
peppermint.

"Mort's going to be fine." I had absolutely
no data with which to support this. They
were the first of the masses to arrive. I
guessed that Sandy had called her sister
and was still home waiting for Gloria to come
help with the children.

"Where is he? What have you done with
him?"

What have I done with him? Like maybe
I had put him in a storage closet? "He's being seen by the doctors now."

"The doctors!" she said. "He's with doctors!"

"This is a hospital."

"Mother, what happened?" Nora said. She was as well-dressed as ever, but looking a little less confident, as if perhaps even she understood her own culpability in the day's events.

"Your father showed up at the flower shop and then Romeo showed up at the flower shop. I wasn't expecting either one of them. They got into a fistfight."

"So your boyfriend did this. You admit it!" Lila said.

"I admit it," I said.

"Nora, you're my witness." She turned to me. "I will sue you, so help me God."

But Nora was falling down in her witnessing duties. She was punching numbers on her cell phone and pacing off across the lobby for privacy. I had a sudden chilling vision of Nora testifying against me in court. She would point me out to the jury, say, That's her. "I don't know what you're going to sue me for exactly. I don't have any money. I wasn't involved in the fight."

Lila was only stumped for a second. "It happened in your store. That means you're liable."

"Well, seeing as how Mort threw the first

pot of flowers, I would say you were liable, if I was the kind of person who sued other people, which I'm not."

"You contemptible bitch," Lila said. "I told Mort this was lunacy, flying across the country to try and straighten out your love life. But he had to help you. He had to be the good guy. This is how you thank him."

"This is how I thank him," I repeated, and then reminded myself of Romeo. "Aren't you a little curious about how he's doing? Don't you want to go and talk to his doctors?"

Lila flashed her blinding incisors at me in something between a growl and a snap. For a second I thought she really did mean to bite me. Then she stomped off. Never did one woman get so much sound out of such a small heel.

"I can't believe you let this happen," Nora sighed when she came back. She watched Lila's retreat to the nurses' station but did not follow. "Alex is on his way over. If she talks about suing again, maybe he can shut her up."

I hit Nora once when she was fifteen. She came home drunk at four in the morning after I had spent the night on the phone with the police and local area morgues. She came in the front door and proceeded up to her bedroom without stopping to say hello. When I called out her name in a mixture of relief, joy, and fury, she told me to drop dead. I slapped her open handed across the face, exactly the way every child psychologist will tell you you must never do. I replayed that scene over in my mind for years, trying to think how I could have handled it differently, properly, but I never came to any other conclusion. It was my failing as a parent, but to this day smacking her seemed like the only logical response to her actions. There in the hospital waiting room I put my hand on her shoulder. "If you want to see your father and his wife, you invite them out to see you. Buy them plane tickets, I don't care. But don't you ever, ever conspire against me with anyone again and expect me to forgive you because I am your mother. I am sick and tired of forgiving you, Nora."

The story of the slap was especially fitting because Nora now wore the same look of utter incredulity that she had worn at fifteen, the red imprint of my hand still fresh on her cheek. "I was trying to *help* you," she said. "I called Daddy so he could talk some sense into you. Clearly Mr. Cacciamani is a dangerous man—don't you understand that now? Do you still think he's so wonderful after what he did to my father?"

"Nora," I said, trying very hard to keep my voice steady, "I think you should go and comfort your stepmother because if I have to talk to you about this for one more minute, I'm going to say something we'll both feel bad about later."

Again with the open mouth, the disbelieving hurt. I was sure I was doing the wrong thing. I could not help it. Not every relationship works out. It hadn't worked out with Mort, it wasn't going to work out with Romeo. Was it possible that it might not work out with Nora? Could I ever come to such a point with a daughter to say "Enough's enough" and "See you around?" The very thought of it made me want to run to her and beg forgiveness, and I might have, had there been time.

God forgive me for what I know to be a small-minded slur against Romeo's family, but when they came in the door I couldn't help but think of *West Side Story,* the Jets walking down the streets of Hell's Kitchen snapping their fingers together in a way that was supposed to establish them as dangerous characters. There were so many of them and they all looked so much alike. The wives all looked like sisters, and though I had met four of his sons before (counting Tony, who was still in Ecuador), I could not tell one from the other. It wasn't like they were twins, mind you, I just couldn't remember which was which. My only lucky break was that the old woman didn't appear to be in attendance. They came toward me in a block, a mass, and while I was ready to defend myself against Lila and Nora, I knew I could not offer the slightest resistance to them. Just as I thought they were going to run me down, stomp me to death, the whole pack veered to the left and went to the nurses' station. There was a flurry of inquiries, some raised voices, and then every last one of them disappeared through the swinging double doors marked NO ADMITTANCE: HOSPITAL PERSONNEL ONLY. That was it.

Two minutes later Father Al came in looking flustered and concerned. "Al," I said, and waved him down.

I could see the confusion on his face. He was trying to place me as a parishioner and then he remembered. "Julie, oh. Julie. Are you all right? Were you hurt?" He patted my hand. It was such a relief to have someone pat my hand.

"No, I'm fine."

"What about Romeo? Raymond called me. He said there was an accident and he said something about you."

I could imagine what the something was, but Al was a priest and wouldn't say. "He's going to be fine, I think. Oh, God, I hope he's going to be fine. There will be some stitches, maybe a broken bone at worst. He got into a fight with my ex-husband."

"Mort? Mort's in town?"

"You know Mort?"

"I don't know him myself, no, but I've heard plenty about him over the years. I certainly feel like I know Mort."

"Well, they ran into each other." I thought of how that sounded, but then decided to let it stand.

"And Romeo's children . . ." He looked around nervously. "Have they come in yet?"

I nodded. "They're already in the back with him. I don't even know if they saw me."

"This is going to be bad," he said. "Romeo will be fine. He's had his share of stitches before. He was such a scrapper when we were in school. I thought he had outgrown it."

"He probably had. He was provoked."

"We'll keep that between us." Al looked toward the doors. "I really should go in there."

"Do me a favor, will you? Let me know how he is. Tell him I'm out here. I know they'll never let me in to see him, but I don't want him to think I just walked away."

"He knows that."

I suddenly felt a great sob come up from my chest, and it got halfway out before there was time to properly suppress it. "I'm absolutely prepared to give him up. I don't mean to sound so melodramatic, but I can't keep causing him all this trouble with his family. I love Romeo. I only want what's best for him—you know that, don't you?"

Al took me in his arms and let me cry on his black shirt for a minute. Gloria would have done the same thing if she hadn't been home with the kids. I pulled myself upright and ran my hands beneath my eyes. "Go on," I said. "I'm fine."

Al nodded and smiled at me, then he went through the doors without even stopping to ask the nurse's permission.

What if Romeo thought I was gone? What if he didn't even know I was out in the lobby? All I wanted was to hold his hand, to tell him everything was going to be fine. I wanted the chance to tell him all sorts of comforting lies about how everything would turn out fine. But once Mort threw that pot of flowers I lost all of my rights, or I realized I'd never had any to begin with.

Sandy came in next. It was starting to feel like a terrible episode of *This Is Your Life*. I felt that if I stood there long enough, my third-grade teacher would come in through the electric doors. "I always thought that Julie Roseman was trouble," she'd say.

"Dad?" Sandy asked me. She looked particularly disheveled and I wondered if she had been working in the garden. There was dirt on the knees of her jeans.

"I don't know. Nora and Lila are back there with him now. I'm afraid I'm persona non grata on both sides. No one has come out to tell me anything."

"Have you asked?"

There hadn't been time, exactly. "I've just been standing here. I don't even know what I'm doing."

Sandy, never a take-charge sort of girl,

went up to the nurse and asked for the status of Mort Roth and Romeo Cacciamani.

"Are you a relative?" the nurse asked. She had seen a lot of relatives.

Sandy told her yes.

"Which one?"

"Both," Sandy said authoritatively. "Roth is my father and Cacciamani is my uncle."

"They're related?"

"By marriage," Sandy said. "Not blood. They hate each other."

"Obviously," the nurse said. She thumbed through some papers and then nodded her head. "Hang on a second." She picked up the phone.

"You go in and see your dad," I said. "I can wait here."

"Is he going to die?"

"Eventually, yes, but not from anything that happened today."

"Then I'll wait with you for a minute. Dad's got Lila and Nora. That's a pretty full house."

I wanted to kiss her. I kissed her. "How are the kids?"

"Their life is a party. They couldn't believe that Gloria was coming over to take care of them. She was going to take them shopping."

"Did you tell them about Mort?"

"I thought I should find out what's going on first. They don't need much information."

"Okay," the nurse said, putting down the phone and making some notes on a pad that said *Prozac* across the top. I wondered where I could get some of those. She looked at me. "You're the ex-wife slash girlfriend, correct?"

"Correct."

"What the hell. It's nothing serious, any-way. Many bruises for both parties. Roth looks like a concussion and two broken ribs. They'll keep him overnight for observation, but he should be out of here with a splitting headache by morning. Cacciamani had eighteen stitches, a broken left wrist, they didn't say which bones, and, coincidentally, two broken ribs. They'll let him go in about an hour." She looked at us both hard. "Is either of these bozos laying a hand on you two?"

"Absolutely not," Sandy said. "I swear."

"Well, watch them."

Sandy and I promised to do that and then we took our places in the chairs. "What a day," I said. "What a horrible, horrible day."

"Do you want to tell me what happened?"

"Not particularly."

"I was just starting to like him a little, the idea of him at least."

"Romeo?"

Sandy nodded.

"That's really nice. I'm giving him up now. This is enough. Nobody needs all of this. My love is going to kill him and I couldn't stand that." I felt like I was going to start crying again. I pointed to the door. "Go back there and see if your father's awake." Mort had ruined my life once again, but I still couldn't help feeling vaguely responsible for his pulverized state. If it wasn't for me, he wouldn't be bleeding now. Of course, if it wasn't for Mort, I wouldn't have been dating to begin with.

Sandy pushed out of her chair. "I'll be back in a minute."

"Take your time," I said. "I'm not going anywhere."

I would have thought I'd be wired like a radio, but in fact I was so tired I thought about stretching out over the chairs and slipping off into a coma. I hoped they would notice me in a day or two and give me a room, hook me up to a nice glucose drip. I couldn't imagine going back to work and I couldn't imagine going home. The hospital seemed like a fine place to set up camp.

There was a pretty waiflike girl with long black hair and a dark purple scarf looped several times around her neck wandering through the waiting room. She would stop in front of people and ask them a question I couldn't hear. They shook their heads and she moved on to the next group. She looked like the gypsy princess in every film that had a gypsy princess. She had those huge, sad eyes and exceptional posture. When she started to walk toward me, I just continued to stare at her like this was a movie.

"Mrs. Roseman?" she asked.

I looked up at her and blinked in agreement.

"I'm Patience Cacciamani."

"Plummy?"

She nodded. She had tiny gold rings on all of her fingers and one of her ears was pierced three times. On her this looked like a good idea. It was easy to imagine her as a fresco painting in a cathedral or a marble statue in the Gardner Museum.

"My dad wanted me to tell you he's okay. He made everybody else go out in the hall so he could talk to me alone. He wants to know if you're okay." She stared at me for a minute, but I wasn't sure what I was supposed to say. "Are you okay?"

I couldn't understand why she was talking to me. That fact was so confusing that I could barely make out her words. "I'm okay."

She sat down in Sandy's chair. "You don't look so great, if you don't mind me saying."

"I don't mind at all."

"It's funny we should meet this way. I had wanted to meet you, but it never occurred to me it would be like this."

"You wanted to meet me?"

"Sure," she said. "Dad's crazy about you."

"But what about your brothers?"

She waved her hand at me, a gesture she had picked up from her father. "They're idiots. Not idiots, really. They're good guys one at a time, but when you put them together they're like, I don't know, like a bunch of moose or something."

This made me smile.

"They won't actually hurt you—I hope you know that—but they do seem to despise you. I don't mean to be rude, but I think we should be able to speak frankly."

Where this child came up with this much

poise was beyond me. It made me want to go out and have a couple more holes put in my ear. "I agree. Absolutely. Tell me about your father."

She stared off into the middle of the waiting room as if she was trying to conjure him in her mind so as to report with complete and impartial accuracy. "Stitches here," she said, and drew a line with her finger across her own temple. I could see the flowerpot landing there now. "And here." She touched her lip. "He broke his wrist, but only one little bone, and there are two cracked ribs." She put a hand beneath her breast and pressed into her ribs. "It must have been one hell of a fight."

"It was that."

"How's the other guy, your ex?"

"I hear he has a concussion. They're keeping him overnight."

"That's good. I don't mean good that he's hurt, but this way all the boys will be able to say Dad won. Dad doesn't have to spend the night."

"That is good."

"It's very difficult for me to understand men's need to hit one another. It's just not something that women do."

I nodded.

"My family has some wicked problem with your family. I think everybody needs to let go of their anger."

"That makes two of us."

"Well, you and Dad like each other. That's a positive start, don't you think?"

"I did think," I said. "But right now it's all a little confusing."

She nodded and gave me a sad smile like the statues of Mary that were everywhere in this town. "I can see that." She looked toward the double doors and sighed. "I guess I should be getting back. They're going to be releasing him soon. We're supposed to take the cars around back and pick him up. It was very nice meeting you."

"You, too. You'll tell your dad I hope he's okay?" Romeo, Romeo. All I wanted was to hold him in my arms.

"I'll tell him," she said. Plummy leaned toward me. At first I thought she was going to kiss me, but she just brushed my cheek with the back of her hand. "You get some rest."

She wasn't two steps away from me when all of her extended family started pouring into the waiting room.

"Plummy!" the big one yelled. "You get the hell away from her."

"Shut up, Joe," Plummy said without the slightest hint of inflection.

They came toward me in a clump.

"I thought I made things clear to you," Joe said, pointing a finger in my direction. His face was red and he was breathing hard. I thought, if he has a heart attack, that will be my fault, too.

"Joe," Plummy said, "do you want me to get Dad out here? Do you want me to wheel him out and have him see you talk to Mrs. Roseman this way?"

"Shut up," he said to his sister.

She walked up to him. She was taller than I had realized at first. She got her face very nearly in his face. "No, you shut up, Joseph." She kept her voice low. "People are staring at you. They're going to throw you out of the hospital. Leave Mrs. Roseman alone, okay? That's what Dad told me to say. Leave her alone, or so help me God, I'm telling."

I wanted to be this girl. I had never in my life possessed one ounce of her confidence.

Joe looked at me one more time, gave me one more point. "You're ruined." He and his pack retreated.

Plummy looked at me and shrugged. "Forget him," she mouthed. Then she added in a bright voice. "Bye, Mrs. Roseman." She joined her group and followed them out the door.

chapter seventeen

It was a very tentative time in my family. The things that had been said in the hospital were put aside. The next afternoon when Mort was released and went back to Nora's, there was an unspoken agreement that we would all play nice. For Mort's sake, and the sake of his horrible headache, there would be no tension, no bickering among us. Even when we were nowhere near him we didn't fight as a measure of our gratitude that things had not been worse. Still, we all understood this arrangement to be a pyramid of crystal glasses balanced on a few silky wisps of spiderweb. Everyone moved slowly and with exaggerated politeness. I waited almost a week before visiting so as not to ruffle any feathers. "Would you like a cup of coffee, Julie?" Lila asked me. "I can make some. It's no trouble."

"Oh, no, but thank you." I stood on the

front steps of Nora's house balancing a casserole dish on my upturned palms. Macaroni
and cheese from scratch. Four cheeses. My
mother's secret recipe. Mort's uncontested
hands-down all-time favorite. I was sure it
would be swirling down the garbage dis-
posal before I got my car started again.

"Don't you want to come in, say hello to
Mort?" It sounded like she was singing the
invitation. Don't you want to come in-n-n-n-
n-n and say hel-l-l-l-oooo?

Actually, I did want to see Mort. I'm not
exactly sure why. Maybe it was because
since the fight I'd felt like everything in the
world had changed and I wondered if he felt
it, too. "Let him get his rest," I said, the polite
thing to say, the thing I knew Lila wanted to
hear. "If he wants to call me later, I'd be glad
to come back over. How is he doing?"

"Oh, the doctor says he's super. When
this is over, he'll never know it happened.
The swelling in his face has gone down a
lot. Really, it's just his ribs that hurt him. He's
a little sore. We should be going home
soon."

She smiled at me, even though no one
was there to see it. I smiled back. That's how
good we were being.

"Mother?" Nora called out. "Is that you?"

"I'm just dropping off a casserole."

"That's so nice. Don't you want to come in?" Nora was wearing shiny black leggings and an ironed white T-shirt. She was off to Pilates class.

"I need to get to work. Tell Mort I hope he feels better." Notice I said "Mort" and not "your father," so as to not make Lila feel excluded. I went down the steps, turned and waved. Nora and Lila stood at the door, waving back at me. What a pretty pack of Stepford Wives we made.

I hadn't talked to Romeo all week. I sent him a get-well card—who knows if he got it? He sent me a note saying that he would call as soon as the dust settled. But this was a Sahara sort of dust. It swirled and blew 365 days a year. In fact, it never settled, not even for a minute. Then every day after that there was another note from him, saying that he loved me, saying that he missed me, saying that he was getting awfully good at writing me letters and wasn't it lucky that it was his left wrist that was broken. I sat on my bed and read them and cried and cried. I was ruining his life, ripping up his family, and getting him punched, and that wasn't the thing to do when you loved someone as much as I loved Romeo. We both knew that the right thing to do was to walk away. I understood how much I loved him then, when I knew I was going to walk away.

I didn't talk about Romeo, though I thought of nothing else. It would have conflicted with the Geneva Accord of Good Manners. At home Sandy was so nice to me, you would have thought I had a terminal illness. She worked harder at the store, harder around the house, harder at school. She arranged for baby-sitters and left fully prepared meals in the refrigerator. In the evenings she took Tony and Sarah over to see Mort, and all her reports were glowing. "He looks fantastic," she said. "You'd hardly know that anything had happened to him."

I imagined the same was true of Romeo. I imagined that everyone was getting back to normal, except for me.

Gloria was helping out all over the place— at home, at work. She had bought a couple of new outfits that she thought would look good in a florist shop, drawstring pants made out of natural hemp and loose linen jackets covered in a cabbage rose print. She looked more like a florist than I ever did. She had gone in with her spare set of keys the night of the fight and cleaned everything up. She swept all the evidence into plastic garbage bags and took them out to the Dumpster.

"You can't keep working for me like this," I said. "It's too much."

"I like it," she said. "I haven't had a job since Buzz and I got married." Buzz owned an insurance company.

"But nothing's wrong with me. Everyone's acting like I'm the one who was in the hospital."

"Well, technically, you were in the hospital. The waiting room is in the hospital. It takes a toll on you." She put down a bucket of baby's breath. "Julie, you've got to call him. You've got to straighten this out."

"Nothing to straighten," I said. "Nothing at all."

"He loves you."

"I'm destroying his life. I won't do it anymore."

And so I continued to make my way through the fog. I spent so much time thinking about things I shouldn't have been thinking about that I completely failed to notice what was going on around me. It was Gloria

who called the obvious to my attention a few
days later.

"Julie?"

"Hmm?"

"There aren't any flowers."

"Hum?"

"Well, you know this is a flower shop, and
people come here to buy their flowers, but
there aren't any flowers coming in. They're
going out fine, but they aren't coming in."

"What?"

She put her hands on my shoulders and
turned me around so that I had to look at
her square in the face. *"There are no flowers."*

I sniffed the air. With a couple of good
sniffs I could take a pretty accurate inventory. Gloria was right. We were down to a
handful of carnations, some leatherleaf
ferns, one bucket of home-grown gladiolus.
"Oh my God."

"I didn't want to tell you. I kept thinking
you'd notice. I kept thinking they'd show
up."

I thought about Mort. *Get on the phone,
yell at somebody.* I ran past Gloria and took
my place at the desk. I called the first number, but there was no one to yell at. The re-

ceptionist put me on hold and left me there for fifteen minutes. When I called again, she sent me back to hold. When I called back a third time, she hung up on me. My second distributor at least did me the courtesy of telling me my account had been canceled before he hung up on me. I called people I used for special occasions and was told they no longer delivered to my neighborhood. I called people I had never used before and was told they were no longer taking on new accounts. I called to check on my order of one thousand gardenias for next Saturday's wedding and was told there was no record of such an order. Everywhere I went I hit a wall, and the walls just kept coming, taller, thicker, and closer together.

"How bad is it?" Gloria said.

"Very bad."

"Very bad like an enormous screwup or very bad like a Cacciamani?"

"The latter."

"You have to call him," Gloria said. "I'll call him. He wouldn't let this happen to you. He doesn't know about it."

"I'm sure you're right," I said. "But Romeo didn't do it, and he's not going to be able to undo it, either. Joe runs a trucking company.

He's got roots in the business that spread all the way to Idaho." I tossed my pencil down on the table. "I'm wrecked," I said. "Simple as that."

"No," Gloria said. She had tears in her eyes. She was taking this hard, as I would take it hard once I was able to grasp what had happened. "You have to fight."

"I can't fight," I said. "I can't keep on fighting. I've lost. I screwed things up enough on my own. This just polishes off what I started."

Gloria sat down on the floor and put her head between her knees. "I think I'm going to be sick."

"That makes two of us."

I put a sign in the window. ON VACATION. I had to make one up. I had never closed the store for a vacation before. Then I left a phone message for the gardenia bride. Poor, poor bride.

I was going to tell Sandy what had happened when I got home, but she was on her way out the door to Nora's with the kids as I was coming in. "Dad's doing really well," she said. "He and Lila are going home in the morning. I'm going to go over and say good-bye. Do you want to come? I know he'd like to see you. He's asked about you a hundred times."

Tomorrow was Sunday. I didn't have to tell her about the shop right now. "I don't think so, honey. It seems like it would be better if I sat this one out."

"Come with us," Sarah said, and held up her arms to be picked up. She had very little interest in walking anywhere. I picked her up.

"You say good-bye to him for me, okay?"

"You'd come if Lila wasn't there," Tony said.

"Probably not. I'm awfully tired tonight." I kissed the kids and helped them into light jackets. "Sandy, ask Nora to come by on her way home from the airport tomorrow. I'd like to talk to her."

"Another family conference?" Sandy asked suspiciously.

"Not exactly. I just think I'm a little out of touch. Ask her to come over in the morning."

After they left I made myself a bag of microwave popcorn for dinner. I sat cross-legged on top of the kitchen counter eating the kernels one at a time and washing it down with a bottle of white wine. When that was over, I went to bed and went to sleep.

It was after ten o'clock when the phone rang, and for a brief instant I was hopeful. But it was Mort.

"Jules? Can you hear me?"

"Sure," I said. "Why are you whispering?"

"Sandy and the kids left a little while ago and everybody is going to bed. I'm down in the kitchen. I told Lila I wanted a glass of milk."

"You hate milk."

"She doesn't know that. Listen, Julie, I was sorry I didn't get to see you to say good-bye. We never seem to do a good job at ending things."

"Yeah, well, I wanted to say I was sorry about your head. I think it was largely your own fault, but I know that if it wasn't for me it wouldn't have happened."

"I threw the pot at the guy."

I was stunned into silence. What he said sounded almost like an admission of something, and that wasn't Mort's style.

"Are you there?" he said.

"I'm here."

"It's just that I've had a lot of time to think, even with my sore brain and everything. I haven't had this much time to think since I had my gallbladder out."

"So what do you think?"

Now Mort was silent, but I was in bed in the dark. I didn't mind waiting. "It's been nice, being back. I've liked seeing the girls so much, seeing Tony and Sarah. You have them all the time, you probably don't even notice, but they're great."

"I notice."

"I just thought if things were more okay between us, then it would be easier for me to come back and see them. We don't have to be in some huge fight all the time, do we?"

I told him we did not.

"That's great, Jules. You're a real trouper. And the Cacciamani stuff—"

"Don't even go there."

"Really, I have to say it. I think the guy's an asshole, but I understand that it's your business. We're all entitled to throw away our own lives, right?"

Sandy must have been working on him in his reduced state. It sounded like the same sort of logic she had come up with. "Don't worry about it, Mort. Romeo and I are through. Nobody bounces back from a fight like that."

"I bounced back," Mort said.

"Well, you're tougher than the rest of us."

Downstairs I heard Sandy and the kids come in the back door.

"Shh, quiet," Sandy said. "Don't wake up Grandma."

"About the store," he said, and I felt my heart freeze inside my chest. "I got a lot of work done before the fight, but you need to see an accountant. I'll pay for it. I know you don't want me to, but that store matters to me a lot. I don't want to see it go under just because you don't know what you're doing."

My eyes filled up with tears. Mort would hear the truth later from one of the girls. As for tonight, let him have a good night's sleep, let him think that Romeo may not be the worst thing in the world, let him get on that plane tomorrow for Seattle. "Okay," I said. I had forgotten to pull the shades down on the windows and now I could see the moon setting off the tender spring leaves on the trees. It was a beautiful thing.

"I don't mean to say you haven't done a good job. You've kept the place afloat. And the flowers look great. It's just the books."

"I understand."

"I should go," he said. "They're going to find me down here. They've kept real tabs on me. You'd think I was an old man."

Then the tears were running down my cheeks. "Good night, Mort," I said.

"Good night, Jules."

When I opened my eyes and looked at the clock, it was ten-thirty in the morning and the room was flooded in light. I had not slept until ten-thirty since I was in junior high school. I leaned over and checked my watch on the nightstand, thinking the clock must be wrong, but it wasn't. I got up, brushed my teeth, and got dressed. It was Sunday morning and the kids were downstairs watching cartoons.

"We kept the volume down," Tony said. "You're sleeping."

I waved to them and wandered into the kitchen. Nora was there at the table with Sandy and they were drinking coffee and talking.

"God, did I oversleep." I rubbed my hands over my face. "I'm sorry I kept you waiting. You should have come up and gotten me."

Nora shook her head. She looked positively happy, as if the past was truly something that could be forgotten. Maybe she was just glad to have gotten rid of her houseguests. "I just walked in from the airport. Besides, you needed to get some rest."

"Did Lila and your dad get off okay?" I got myself a cup of coffee and joined them.

"Not a hitch. Dad even made a fuss about carrying his own suitcase."

"Good," I said. "That's good."

"So now life gets back to normal," Nora said. She reached over and gave me an uncharacteristic squeeze on the wrist.

I looked at both my girls, smart and good-looking girls, girls who I loved even as they drove me insane. I wanted to remember them in the last peaceful moment I was going to see for a while. "Not exactly."

Both of them set their coffee cups down. They clicked against the table at the exact same instant. "I knew it," Sandy said.

"It's Roseman's," I told them slowly because I didn't want to repeat myself. "There were a lot of problems to begin with."

"What happened?" Sandy said. The two words were like heavy stones thrown off the side of a building.

"All our flowers have been cut off. I've called every supplier I could think of. No one will deliver to us anymore."

"How is that possible?" Nora asked.

"Cacciamani," Sandy said. "They've ruined us. That's it, isn't it? They've frozen us out."

"I don't know that," I said.

"But that's it, isn't it?" Sandy stood up from the table and walked over and closed the kitchen door so Tony and Sarah wouldn't hear us. "You know what's happened. You can figure this out."

"I can figure it out."

I wouldn't have expected this. Sandy was ready to toss the kitchen table through the window, but Nora was just sitting there staring into her coffee cup. "We'll get around it," Sandy said. "We are not going down over this. I don't care if I have to drive to New Hampshire every morning and bring the flowers back myself. They are not going to close us down."

"I don't know," I said.

"I know!" Sandy said, and hit the table with her fist. "Damn it, Mother, snap out of it. You're going to have to fight them."

"We don't have to fight them," Nora said, taking a sip of her coffee. "We already won."

Sandy stopped and looked at her sister. She pulled her hair back behind her ears.

"How did we win?" I said.

Nora didn't look smug. I'll give her that much. There was nothing self-congratulatory in her tone. She just laid out the facts like she would on any other deal she had closed. She was a powerful businesswoman, my older daughter. I forgot that sometimes. "I bought the Cacciamanis' building. I did some research. It turns out they never owned the place. They had rented it all these years. They had a great deal. A classic old Somerville deal where the owner seemed to forget they were there and never raised the rent."

"You bought the building?" Sandy said, sitting back down in her chair.

"I sent them the eviction notice yesterday. They have two weeks to get out. The way I see it, they probably don't have anything saved. There are too many kids for that. They'll never be able to find another place for what they were paying. They'll stumble, they'll fall, they'll never get up."

"Jesus," Sandy said. "I hope you never get that mad at me."

"It's business," Nora said.

I listened to her calculations. What surprised me was that I didn't feel angry at Nora. I had to be fair. If I could see the reasoning behind Joe Cacciamani's attempt to destroy me, then I had to be able to see the logic of Nora bringing down Romeo. This was where we had come to. This was who we were.

"Come on," I said. "Get the kids and get in the car."

"Where are we going?" Sandy said.

"The Cacciamanis'."

"I'm not going," Nora said calmly, and put both hands around her coffee cup as if that would anchor her there.

"We're all going," I said. "All of us together. This is the last absolute dictate I will issue as your mother, but you are going."

Nora sat there for a minute and thought it over. I thought there was going to be a fight. Instead she walked to the sink, rinsed out her cup, and dried her hands. "All right," she said.

"Why do we have to go?" Tony said from the other room.

"Because there aren't any adults to stay home with you," Sandy said.

"Who are these people again?"

"Friends of Grandma's," she said. "Sort of."

chapter eighteen

Somerville, like Rome, was a city built on seven hills. I lived in Spring Hill. Romeo lived in Winter Hill. I had been to his house once before, years ago during the whole Sandy and Tony affair. There had been two meetings, one at our house, one at theirs. He lived on Marshall Street. I remembered it clearly.

"What are you going to say?" Nora asked. Her car had been parked behind mine, so she was driving and I was in the front seat giving directions. Sandy and Tony and Sarah were in the back.

"I just want to tell them it's over. All the fighting, the undermining. The Roseman family is now officially out of the game."

"What about the building?" Nora said. "I've closed on it. I can't give it back."

"Then you'll rent to them. You'll give it to them. I don't know. You'll figure it out. All I know is that I want us to be a certain kind of people. I want us to be decent people." I felt a sense of lightness in my chest. In Somerville the irises and peonies were blooming with mad abandon. Everything felt so easy all of a sudden. We may not get our heart's desire, but we could all be decent people. It absolutely had to be the answer.

Sandy was quiet in the backseat. Tony was reading all the street signs to Sarah. Sandy must have been to this house before. She must have sneaked in a back door, an open window in the dark.

On Marshall Street I told Nora to slow down. I was looking at all the houses. "It's up there on the left," Sandy said. "The one with the balloons on the mailbox."

"Balloons!" Sarah said. Sarah was mad for balloons.

"Maybe they were expecting us," Nora said.

There was definitely something up at the Cacciamanis'. We had to drive all the way around the block to find a parking space.

"Couldn't we do this later?" Nora said. "When they aren't having a party maybe?" She put the car in reverse and worked into the tight spot.

"We'll never come back. You're right, the

timing isn't great, but I really think it's now or never." Even if we were interrupting something, we were doing so in the name of peace. They'd be happy to hear they hadn't lost their store. That fact alone would counteract our presence at their party.

"Never is not a bad option," Nora said.

"Do we have a present?" Tony asked.

"Sort of," Nora said, and opened up her door. "It's called real estate."

Sandy and Nora and I made slow time up the block. Tony and Sarah kept racing ahead and then coming back for us.

"Come on, come on," they yelled, most likely figuring that where there were balloons there was usually cake. I figured we had almost no shot at the cake.

The house was a double-decker with four units. It was a house that was meant to manage a large Catholic family. On one door there was a wreath of flowers, pink and white roses all the way around. It was so simple, so utterly charming, I knew it had to be Romeo's. My heart rose and sank a hundred times just going up the walk.

"I don't know about this," Sandy said quietly.

"Thank you," Nora said.

"Are we going in or what?" Tony said. He ran ahead and pushed the doorbell three times and then ran back and stood behind us. The way we froze to the sidewalk, you would have thought he had pulled the pin out of the grenade.

"Mother," Nora said. "If you're trying to teach me a lesson about taking responsibility for my actions, I have now learned it. Turn around with me and start running like hell."

I was about to agree when a tan young man I didn't recognize swung open the door. He was wearing a pink paper hat that had *90!* sticking out of the top. He had a beard and was wearing Birkenstocks, shorts, and a World Health Organization T-shirt. He looked at us for one second and then made what can only be described as a high-pitched sound of almost unbearable happiness. He ran to Sandy and picked her up by the waist. He swung her around and kissed her neck. He said her name over and over again.

"Do we know him?" Tony said.

"He was a friend of your mom's a long time ago," Nora told him.

Tony Cacciamani put my daughter down.

"My God," he said. "How did you even know I was back? I only got here two hours ago."

"I didn't know," Sandy said. She put her hands on his chest. "Are you okay?"

"I'm fine. I'm so good now. You look so beautiful. You're all grown up." He looked at the rest of us. "Hey, Mrs. Roth. Hey, Nora."

"Hi, Tony," I said. I didn't know that Tony knew Nora. For the first time it occurred to me that my older daughter must have helped my younger daughter plan her trysts.

"And who are you?" he said to Tony and Sarah. "Nora, are they yours?"

"Mine," Sandy said. There was, of course, some embarrassment in the introductions. When she had named her son Tony Anderson, she hadn't seen Tony Cacciamani in years and figured she probably never would again.

"Hello," Tony said, shaking their hands. His voice was more serious now.

"Sandy's been divorced for three years," Nora said. "Let's just skip right ahead to that."

Tony brightened right back up and invited us inside. For once I was grateful for Nora's directness. "You came for my grandmother's birthday party? Man, things really have changed since I've been gone."

"It's Mrs. Cacciamani's birthday?" I said.

Tony nodded his pink hat and put his arm casually around Sandy's shoulder, as if it had never left that spot. "Ninety today."

The living room was packed with Italians in party clothes, every one of them wearing pink paper hats with *90!* sticking out of the top. There were tables full of sandwiches and vegetable trays. There was punch in a bowl the size of a large fish tank. There was a pink-and-white sheet cake that took up one whole card table. In the corner there was an accordion player grinding through "That's Amore!" It was one hell of a party. Everywhere I looked people were laughing and drinking. No one seemed to notice we were there. I plowed into the room looking for Romeo and everyone I passed smiled and tried to scoot over to give me enough room to get through. They were regular people, decent people, just like we were.

"Have you seen Romeo?" I said to a little boy at the punch table.

"I think he's in the kitchen," he said, and pointed. "That way."

I thanked him and pressed on. I had lost

my family in the crowd. I worked my way to the kitchen door.

Plummy and her father were struggling with a bag of ice that had frozen together. The *90!s* on their paper hats were touching. He didn't look especially happy. There was a neat line of stitches in his forehead and near his lip just the way Plummy had described them. There was a plaster cast on his wrist.

It was the moment I was most afraid of. I was afraid that he would not be glad to see me. I waited, taking a sad pleasure in watching him when he didn't know I was there. I wondered if it was the last time I would ever see him. "Romeo," I said.

But Romeo looked up and when he saw me his mouth fell open and for a second he seemed to be caught just between laughing and sobbing. He smiled at me like his son had smiled at Sandy. He said my name over and over as if he wanted to hear the sound of it. He came to me and hugged me to him. He kissed me, held me out from him to look at me, then he kissed me again. "My God, you're here!"

"I've got to straighten things out, with you,

with your family." I wanted to be serious and brave. I wanted to melt into him forever.

"I'm going to take this out to the living room," Plummy said, scooping the ice back into the bag. She smiled at me on her way out. "Hi, Mrs. Roseman."

"I love that girl," I said to Romeo. "I didn't get the chance to tell you that before."

He kissed me gently, because of his lip. The kitchen door swung shut, swung open. Two young men I didn't know walked in. By the expressions on their faces you would have thought they had caught us dissecting Junior, the family dog.

"Julie," Romeo said with some hesitation. "These are my sons. This is Alan and this is Nicky. Nicky came all the way from Germany with his family for the party."

"Julie Roseman?" Nicky said. Alan went back through the door.

In half a minute they were all there. I could hear Nora's voice rise above the others in the living room. Then we were all back in the living room and everyone's voice seemed to go up. The accordion player stopped in the middle of his song and the last note dangled for a moment in the air and then faded.

"Rosemans!" I heard the old woman yell.

"There are Rosemans in my house!" We were easy to spot. We were the ones without hats.

"Oh, dear God," I said. "I'm sorry, I'm sorry." I turned to Romeo. "Listen to me, this is so important. I would never have come otherwise. I know about your store, the lease."

Romeo put his eyebrows down. "Let's do this later," he whispered.

"What about the lease?" Raymond said.

I was looking for Tony and Sarah. I wanted to make sure they were all right. They were wearing hats, picking icing roses off the side of the cake with three other children who they would probably grow up to hate some-day. Nobody knew they were Rosemans. Nobody cared about them.

"Nora bought your building."

"*Your* Nora bought it?" Romeo said.

At the mention of her name, Nora squared her shoulders and came across the room. "I'm Nora Bernstein," she said. "I bought the building."

"You evicted us?" Romeo said.

"She evicted us?" Raymond said.

"I was going to tell you after the party,"

Romeo told his son. "I didn't know who bought it."

"Get them out of my house!" the old woman screamed. She was wearing a blue pantsuit and had a pink paper hat that was bigger than everyone else's. It said *I'm 90!* on the top. I couldn't believe they got it on her. She was pretty far away from me, which gave me some peace of mind.

"Come on," Raymond said, and put a hand on Nora's arm. "Let's go." Nora stared at him until he took it away.

"I bought it because I was trying to protect my mother. You cut off all her flowers. She's ruined because of you." This was less than true, since Nora had bought the building before she knew about the flowers, but she should be allowed to keep her dignity.

"I cut off her flowers?" Romeo said. "What are you talking about?"

"We don't need to get into that," I said to Nora.

"Yes we do. You said this is honesty time." She turned around to the crowd and clapped her hands three times. "Listen up, people. There's going to be a game at this party. It's called True Confessions. I bought Romeo's flower shop and evicted him. He contacted every flower distributor in the area to cut off my mother's supply and ruin her business."

The crowd collectively inhaled at this piece of information.

"Wait a minute," Romeo said. "I never did that."

Joe lumbered forward from the crowd. His *90!* hat seemed barely bigger than a folded Kleenex sitting on his head. I wondered if he had ever owned a shirt that could be buttoned at the neck. "I did that," he said. "She'll never get her hand on another flower as long as I live."

"You ruined her?" Romeo stepped toward his son. "You blackballed her?"

"You were right, Mom," Nora said. "This is so much better."

I took Romeo's arm. "It went both ways. That's the whole point. We have to stop this right now."

"Come in the kitchen," Romeo said to me, then he raised his voice in the crowd. "Cacciamanis, Rosemans, in the kitchen. No cousins, no kids. Mother, in the kitchen."

"I'm not going in there with them," she said.

Nora went over and whispered something

in her ear. The old woman looked furious but followed us in.

"How did you do that?" I whispered to Nora.

"I told her she wasn't allowed in the kitchen."

Tony and Sandy were already in there. I don't know how they had managed that. They were sitting at the table holding hands. The night he had tried to take her out of her bedroom window fifteen years ago they had sat on our living room couch, rain-soaked and crying, holding hands the same way. They looked surprised to see us.

"That's the girl! That's the one!" the old woman said. "Get her off of Tony."

Romeo held his hand up to his mother. "Hang on a minute. So Joe, you went behind my back to ruin Roseman's?"

"She had it coming."

"Out," he said.

"What?"

"Out of my house." Romeo stood with his feet apart and his arms crossed over his chest. It was a stance that meant business.

The point was to figure out how to make peace between Cacciamanis and Rosemans, not stir up trouble between the Cacciamanis. The last thing I wanted to do was separate Romeo from his thuggish firstborn. "No," I said. "You can't do that. We're going to fix this."

"Don't you tell my father no," Joe said. He pointed a finger at me, and I wondered if he had inherited his grandmother's inclination toward poking.

"Christ," Nora said. "This never ends."

"We just need to stop it," I said, my voice sounding a little frantic. "We need to make an agreement once and for all. If you and I can't see each other anymore, I can accept that, but I don't want to live like crazy people."

"We can't see each other?" Romeo said. He looked at me as if such a horrible outcome had never occurred to him before. I thought at that moment I would cry for loving him so much.

"At least you've got that straight," said one of the sons—who knew which one?

Plummy, who was wearing a little lavender sundress with a black cardigan sweater, clapped her hands together. She was clearly ready to make order out of chaos. "Okay," she said. "Once and for all we're going to get to the bottom of this and then we're going back to the party." She looked at her brother Tony, who smiled hugely.

"Plummy, this is Sandy," he said.

"Hi, Sandy," Plummy said, and leaned over to shake her hand. "Now somebody here knows this story." She bit her lip and looked around the room as if she hadn't quite made up her mind who to call on first. She gave me a look, then my daughters, her father, and each of her brothers. "Grammy," she said finally. "What's the story?"

"The Rosemans are pigs," she said.

"Okay, that's a start. Now, why are the Rosemans pigs?"

That was the question. When you boiled everything down to the lowest common denominator, why were Rosemans pigs? Why were the Cacciamanis slimy fish? I assumed my parents knew the answer, but they were both dead. Mort didn't know. I didn't know.

"Come on," Plummy said.

"It's my birthday," the old woman said. She reached up and touched her hat as if to drive her point home. Unlike many members of the party, she had had the good sense to put her elastic strap in the back.

"Happy birthday," Plummy said. "Everybody wants to eat the cake and watch you open your presents, but that isn't going to happen until you fess up."

"I want to go now." She was trying to pass herself off as feeble, but it didn't wash.

"I'm really sorry," Plummy said, somehow sounding genuinely sorry. "But you can't go until you tell us what happened. We've all waited long enough." The clear fact was that Plummy Cacciamani was the one who ruled this world. She was a kind and modest dictator, no doubt, but she was a dictator nonetheless.

"I don't know anything," she said. "Don't you believe these lying Rosemans."

"You don't know anything?" Plummy asked.

The old woman looked away from her. "Nothing about them. Who'd want to know about Rosemans?"

It was not a particularly warm day, but it was becoming a warm kitchen by the minute. Cacciamanis tried very hard not to brush shoulders with Rosemans, except for Tony and Sandy, who were inching their chairs closer and closer together. I was pressed against an ancient gas stove and hoping no one would think to reach over and turn it on.

"What about the letters?" Plummy said, as if this was one possibility.

"What letters?"

Plummy looked like the very picture of innocence. She reached up and twisted one of the gold hoops in her ear. "The letters under your mattress. The ones in the pink silk handkerchief. The ones that all start 'My Darling . . .' "

The eldest Cacciamani turned with flames in her eyes. She raised a finger to poke, but Plummy gently pushed it down. Everyone shifted to make sure they had a very clear view of the action. "Why are you reading my letters?"

"I clean your room, Grammy. I flip your mattress every month. I never thought it mattered before, but now I think it does."

I was very impressed to think that Plummy would turn the mattress every month. I managed to do it maybe once a year. Who still hid things under the mattress? The old lady probably kept all her money in a sock.

"They're none of your business." Grammy Cacciamani was gasping a little now. Her eyes searched the kitchen counters, and I wondered if she was looking for tiny nitro-glycerine tablets.

"I know that," Plummy said calmly. "That's why I never mentioned them before. But now we have this problem."

The old woman took a deep breath and thought it over for a minute. She leaned against the refrigerator, which was covered in children's drawings. She looked trapped. "I'll tell you later," she said.

Plummy went and put her arm around her grandmother. She kissed the old woman's cheek. "You tell me later and I'll just have to get everybody together again so I can tell them what you said. Tell me now," she whispered kindly.

We were all waiting, five sons, three wives, my two girls, Plummy, me and Romeo. Mattresses? Letters? We leaned toward her mesmerized. Nobody said anything. Only two people were allowed to talk now, the oldest Cacciamani and the youngest. The oldest didn't say a word and Plummy waited, letting her grammy twist in the wind. If this was a test of wills, I had no idea who was more likely to break.

"Come onto the porch," the old woman said weakly.

Plummy nodded her head and patted the old woman's hand as if she was the police interrogator who knew a signed confession was on the way. She led her grandmother past the rest of us and out onto the back porch. The accordion started up again in the other room. We waited.

"How's your head?" I asked Romeo.

"Stupid," he said. "My head is stupid."

"Does it hurt anymore?"

"Nah, just the ribs a little when I breathe. How about Mort?"

I told him that Mort had healed up and gone home to Seattle this morning.

Romeo smiled. "That guy has a hell of an arm."

We waited and waited. In the other room people had started laughing again. They had forgotten about us. They had forgotten about the birthday. They were there for a party and it didn't matter whose party it was. Finally Raymond went and looked out the back window.

"Can you see anything?" Romeo asked.

"Grammy's in the chair and Plummy's kind of leaning over her. It looks pretty intense. I can't see what they're saying."

"I don't know why we have to shake her down on her birthday," Alan said. His pretty Italian wife stood next to him, nodding.

"Because we're not going to come back and do this again next week," Nora said. "It isn't that much fun."

It occurred to me that if the old woman didn't give her secret up to Plummy, she would have to take on Nora in the next round. It would be a different kind of shakedown altogether.

"What letters?" Tony said.

"Wait, wait!" Raymond pulled back from the window. "She's coming in."

I imagine that I now have some idea of how the defendant feels when the jury files back into the courtroom with a folded-up piece of paper. Plummy came back alone. She pulled her hair away from her face and twisted it into a knot, which miraculously held itself in place without the aid of pins.

"Where's Grammy?" Raymond said.

"She's sitting down outside for a minute. She wanted some air."

"So what's the story?" Nora said. Nora, more than anyone else, wanted to get the hell out of there.

"The story is this." Plummy leaned back against the counter and spread out her arms behind her. She spoke to Nora. "My grand-

mother and your grandfather had a love affair."

"My grandfather?" Nora pointed at her
chest.

"The hell they did," Joe said.

Plummy held up her hand but didn't look
at him. "Please," she said. "This was a very
long time ago. The Rosemans had their shop
in Somerville and Grammy and Grampy had
a shop in the North End. Grammy met Mr.
Roseman buying vases and they fell in love.
I guess it was all pretty hot. Grammy wanted
to be closer to Mr. Roseman, so she talked
Grampy into moving their shop to
Somerville. She told him it was a better place
to raise children. Daddy was three years old
then and they called the place Romeo's. The
way I understand it, Mr. Roseman strung
Grammy along big-time. He kept promising
Grammy that he was going to run away with
her, but every time she was ready to go, he
would come up with some lame excuse and
they never did it. After a while Grammy got
really angry, and I guess she started doing
things to the Rosemans. She said it started
out small at first—she'd bad-mouth their
flowers to other people, she threw a rock
through their window once. Then she hid a

dead fish in their storeroom, a flounder. That was when Mr. Roseman got mad at her and he paid a kid to dump a box of fleas in their store. It was back and forth, one thing and then another. Grammy told Grampy that the Rosemans were trying to ruin them to get their customers, that the Rosemans were trying to force them out of the neighborhood and that they had to fight back. Who knows what Mr. Roseman told Mrs. Roseman? No one actually got ruined until now. There were some other details, but I think that's pretty much the story."

"And they fell for it?" Nora asked her. "My grandmother and old man Cacciamani? They just picked up the feud and ran with it without any more information than that?"

"Well, all of us did, too. Our families hated each other, and we didn't even have the fleas to deal with."

"You expect me to believe that?" Raymond said.

"Go ask her. She's told it once now, I bet she'll tell it again. Or go and read the letters under the mattress. They're pretty steamy."

"But she hated Mr. Roseman," Nicky said. "She hated him more than any of them."

"That's the way it works sometimes,"

Plummy said thoughtfully. "Big love makes for big hate."

"I still hate him," old Mrs. Cacciamani said. She was standing at the door, suddenly looking older than ninety. Her blue pantsuit was wrinkled. Her party hat was tipped to one side. *I'm 90!* it reminded us. "And I'll hate every last one of them until I die."

My father? I thought. My father and the Wicked Witch of the West? The woman he hated above all other life-forms? I could still hear his voice clearly in my head. I could hear every terrible name he called her. Of all the possible explanations, I had to admit this one seemed the most implausible to me.

"Mama, are you sure about this?" Romeo asked.

"Of course I'm sure about this. What do you think, I don't know who I was in love with?" Then, with the surprising vigor of a woman in love, she slammed through the kitchen door and back into her party. It swung open, shut, open, shut, behind her.

The rest of us stood there listening to the accordion music coming through the wall.

"Just to recap," Nora said, taking a drink from a cup of red punch that was sitting on the counter. "What this means is that the birthday girl was in love with my grandfather, my mother is in love with your father, and my sister is in love with Tony here."

Sandy looked mortified.

"That's what it's looking like," Plummy said.

Nora continued. "So the basis of this tedious, never-ending fight is that three generations of Cacciamanis and Rosemans have been in love with each other."

The room took a moment to digest this piece of information. Then Nora started to laugh and pretty soon Sandy was laughing, too. Then Plummy joined in. She put her hand over her mouth, but she was laughing. At that point none of the rest of us got the joke.

"Mr. Cacciamani," Nora said. "Keep your store. Think of me as your benevolent landlord. You," she said, pointing to Joe. "Turn the delivery service back on for my mother's flowers tomorrow. Now I want very much to get out of here. I'm taking my car." She looked at me and Sandy. "Something tells me you two will find rides home."

epilogue

The story ends with a wedding, right?
These stories practically have to. This wedding was on the first of July. Some people
said it was awfully quick, but once they
heard the whole story, they had to agree it
was, in fact, a long time coming. There were
no peonies that late in the summer, but the
roses were fantastic. We're talking garden
roses, not the kind you buy in stores. When
we were done, it looked like we had gotten
our hands on every rose in Massachusetts.
Romeo and I did the whole thing together.
That was how we got the idea of combining
our stores in the first place. We worked together like a dream. I made the bride's bouquet. I had long been liberated from the idea
of white. Every color I could find went into
that bouquet. It was even better than the one
I had made when I married Mort. The wedding was in my backyard. We had a justice

of the peace so that no one would get their toes stepped on religion-wise, but Father Al was there and I saw him moving his lips. Nora was the maid of honor. She insisted on the title. She said she couldn't bear to be anybody's matron of honor. Joe was the best man. Tony and Sarah did the rings and the flowers. It was a small wedding, except that no Cacciamani wedding could ever really be considered small.

Tony and Sandy went to the Cape for their honeymoon. Not exactly Jamaica, but they were saving money to buy a house. For the time being they are living with me. I have more room.

What everyone was asking at the wedding was when were Romeo and I going to get married. Gloria all but demanded an answer. But for us it isn't such an issue. We'd never get all of his family and all of my family into one house, anyway. We're together, trust me on that. The rest of it will fall into place over time. We keep a little apartment that none of the kids know about. It's an efficiency, a third-floor walk-up. It isn't a whole lot bigger than the bed we dragged into it. We've got two cups there, a corkscrew, a couple of old comforters for when it's really cold, some towels. It doesn't take much to make a place feel like home. To anyone who ever thought that love and passion were for the young, I say, Think again. I am speaking from personal experience here.

Romeo says we live together at work. Most couples work apart but live in one house. We're just doing it the other way around. Things have gotten busy now that we're doing the wedding and party-planning service. It turns out we actually need all the various family members we've got on the payroll. We're always at the same store, one day his, one day mine. The next thing we knew, they were both ours. It's Romeo and Julie's now. Two locations to better serve you.

acknowledgments

I am glad to have this opportunity to thank Kay Horton and Pony Maples for parties and pictures; the Bates family and Lonnie Fuqua for telling me how to arrange the flowers; Karl VanDevender, Jeannine Hopson, Wendy Hill, and Pam Roberts for picking up my slack at work and for being so upbeat and supportive.

No one could find a better agent than Lisa Bankoff or a more insightful editor than Shaye Areheart. I feel lucky to have them both.

My most heartfelt thanks is for the home team: my mother, Eve Wilkinson, my husband, Darrell Ray, my daughters, Heather Nancarrow and Ann Patchett, dear Robb and Marcie Nash, and my best friend, Gloria Knuckles, whom no amount of fictionalization could disguise.

about the author

Jeanne Ray works as a registered nurse at the Frist Clinic in Nashville, Tennessee. She is married and has two daughters. Together, she and her husband have ten grandchildren. This is her first novel.

ℓ